ODDS INTO ENDS

by

Regina A. McIntyre

"ODDS INTO ENDS" by Regina A. McIntyre.

Dedicated to my wonderful family

with God's Blessing on

each and every one of the

witty, good-humored, enterprising,

and, thank God,

healthy individuals.

Life is a dream for the wise,

a game for the fool,

a tragedy for the poor.

- Sholom Aleichem

CHAPTER 1

COLD AND WINDY

She stood on her toe-tips to get a cup of water to rinse her mouth after brushing her teeth. She could barely reach the faucet of the huge kitchen sink. The radio in the living room made the gloomy announcement: Punxsutawney Phil, the famous weather gopher, who never fails to rise from his hole-in-the-ground home every February 2nd, had seen his shadow. There would be six more weeks of winter ahead in Philadelphia.

"Will you hurry? You're going to be late for Mass!" Her mother laid the serrated knife alongside the cutting board on the kitchen table. The onions were diced and ready to be added to the Sunday morning omelet. She looked forward to some quiet time. The next hour would allow her to reflect on the scripture, and maybe there would be time to squeeze in a Rosary.

"I'm hurrying!" She jammed her feet into the loafers and straightened her skirt. Bracing herself against the early morning chill, she zipped her anorak and wrapped her scarf around her mouth and nose.

"Zostańczie z Bogum" *("Stay with God"),* she called out to her mother. The sound of her voice was muffled.

"Idź z Bogum!" *("Go with God!")* replied her mother, almost automatically.

Parishioners were beginning to fill the pews for the early 7:00 a.m. service at St. Agnes Church, the most popular of the several masses offered every Sunday. These early church-goers were eager to fulfill their weekly obligation on their 'day of rest' and hurry home for a big breakfast and a leisurely look at the newspapers, the Sunday *Record* or the Sunday *Inquirer*, depending on which paper carried their favorite 'funnies.'

In the dark, candlelit hallows of St. Agnes, the statue of St. Joseph stood on the auxiliary altar of the left aisle. Tall and handsome, he watched over the congregation with a kind, paternal countenance. The foster father of Jesus held a significant place in Jeanie Szymborska's young heart. He was her 'go-to person' whenever she was in trouble or just aching for love.

The little *Bushas* of the Third Order were gathered in the pews facing St. Joseph, rosary beads flashing through their rough, red fingers. Their hushed and mumbled utterings of Hail Marys offered a softly audible mantra that was soothing to the soul. Beneath the statue of St. Joseph, a metal cart displayed six rows of votive candles; only a few of them were lit. A coin box was conveniently placed at the base to accept donations for the lighting of a candle.

One of the *Bushas*, prayer beads securely tucked within her left palm, rose from her seat and leaned heavily on her cane. She shuffled her way into the aisle and proceeded toward the statue. Parishioners waiting in line respectfully pulled back and allowed her to go first. She lowered herself onto the kneeler by gripping the bars of the unsteady frame. From her sweater pocket, she pulled out a coin and slipped it into the slot. She lit three candles.

Jeanie watched her from her seat in the second row of the left aisle, and wondered if this old woman ever had a life? Was she ever as young as herself? Jeanie knew old people were looked upon by others as clumsy and stupid, but that's not really who she thought they were. She explored the possibility of one day getting to know one of these saintly ladies. *I'll get to talk to her and learn about a time and events I can't even imagine.*

Jeanie settled in, made a silent "good morning' prayer, and bookmarked the daily readings in the Sunday Missal. She stared up at the familiar icon painted on the wall above the statue of St. Joseph. The image depicted a dove, using her beak to tear open her chest and send forth blood to feed the young chicks gathered about her, their hungry little mouths open wide in expectation.

The icon was as old as the church itself. At ten years old, Jeanie had no concept of metaphor. The image made her feel uncomfortable; however, she was drawn to it at every mass. Maybe it was a convenient distraction from Father York's homilies that constantly berated his parishioners for the sinners they were.

Her mother, Josephine, was divorced and therefore, duly excommunicated from the church, a situation that weighed heavily on her shoulders, because her cradle Catholicism was birthed in Poland, where ethnicity and faith were synonymous.

Jeanie had no recollection of her parents' relationship or why a divorce would separate one from the church. She was fed and sheltered, and she loved life, school, the church, and friends. And, perhaps most of all, she loved reading Alexander Dumas' classic novel, *"The Count of Monte Cristo."*

Her father had abandoned them when she was only six months old.

Either from guilt, or because of a genuine interest in her daughter's spiritual upbringing, Josephine made it her mission to involve herself with her daughter Jeanie's emergence into the dogmatic Catholic faith. She resolutely went on with the tutoring of the required catechism, attending mass every week, regardless of how it challenged her self-image.

Proud and assertive, Josephine did her best to maintain her dignity, as well as her seat, when the call to communion came. The parishioners seated near her would respond to the bell by jostling their way past her on their way to the altar rail.

The Sunday Jeanie took her first communion, clothed in the white dress of purity and the veil of faith, was the last Sunday that Josephine attended mass. Once she saw the accomplishment of her mission fulfilled, her fledgling was on her own.

The parish of Saint Agnes enveloped approximately seven square miles in North Philadelphia, not far from Center City. It stretched west from the Delaware River for ten blocks. The neighborhood was primarily blue-collar, a medley of Eastern European immigrants and first-generation citizens.

Saint Agnes, being a Roman Catholic church, was predominantly Czechoslovakian, with a smattering of Polish and German families. The Polish language shared some similarity with Slovak, and Germany had invaded both countries often enough to have its tongue adopted as a second language. The structure was small, as far as churches go. There was nothing grandiose about its appearance, just gray quarry stone of a single story with an approximate ten-foot ceiling height; a sturdy building with a stone cross embedded, centered of its A-frame roof.

The double doors of the entrance were constructed of heavy oak wood, which required a strong arm to open. Fortunately, for the elderly, there were no steps to climb.

Within the flexible boundaries of the parish was the establishment of the two other ethnic faiths. St. George provided the Eastern Orthodox faith to the Rumanian culture on Brown Street, four blocks away. Two streets up from St. Agnes, the imposing structure of the Russian Orthodox Church completed the ethnic and religious diversity of this Christian community. The Jewish Synagogue was on Fourth and Market Streets, just outside of the neighborhood range.

Philadelphia was a city of row homes built by masons and tons of bricks. Most of the homes were built in the early years of the twentieth century to house the recent immigrants who brought their crafts and skills to the growing industrial economy. The city was a delightful hodgepodge of nationalities from Eastern Europe.

After mass, Jeanie made a dash for the bakery across the street to claim a spot in line. Poppy Seed Loaf was a special Sunday treat that Josephine allowed her to indulge in for breakfast. It was just three years into the Second World War, and fourteen years after the start of the Great Depression. Jeanie understood that money was tight for her single mother.

Valentine Pancross had overslept - as usual. Saturday nights were spent reveling at the Slovak Social Club, across the street from the home of the widowed Stefcha Goniek. Valentine enjoyed free room and board there. He also enjoyed *carte blanche* at the social club.

Valentine entertained the members with his rich baritone voice. His wit and good looks served him well.

On this wintry, cold Sunday morning, he was stumbling down the stairway, still not fully awake; there'd be no mass for him, breakfast was his goal, along with a good hot cup of coffee. Walter was making his way up the steps; they crossed paths at the landing.

"Mom's good and pissed!"

"What for…what about?"

"Does the name Elsa mean anything to you?" A nasty snicker trailed behind him.

Val's jaw tightened; his complexion blanched; an audible swallow betrayed his immediate angst.

Walter continued his trek up the steps. Val remained rooted to the spot. An array of emotions ran through him: fear, disbelief, anger. As he tried to sort out the dynamics of the situation, he heard Walter titter over the banister, and his gut reaction focused on anger.

In the downstairs hall, he heard the emotional dialogue that was going on in the kitchen. Walter's wife, Marian, was acting as intermediary.

"Give him a chance to explain himself. Manya loves to gossip, and she doesn't always get it right… just so long as the story is juicy."

"There's enough evidence to back up her story," Stefcha's words were laden with exasperation, "In the last two weeks, he's been playing cards till two and three o'clock in the morning. That's a new pastime for him."

It was out in the open; Val would have to address the issue. Dodging twisted corners was a way of life for him. He had entered this particular twist with Elsa in his usual cavalier manner. If there was something to enjoy, then why deprive yourself?

Val felt his heart palpitating, his mouth was dry, he broke out in a sweat; his body was reacting to the rush of adrenaline coursing through his veins. What possibly could have gone wrong?

There wasn't even a hint of the possibility that someone might have seen him with Elsa. The intriguing liaison began less than two weeks ago, and never on a weekend. People were sleeping at that time of night; earning the daily bread was a matter of serious priority. Val didn't have time to work things out; Walter might come downstairs at any moment and goad him into a showdown with Stefcha.

He feigned a stumble as he approached the kitchen, *"Psia krew!"* he uttered.

The conversation ended abruptly, and the immediate silence was ominous. He pulled up his shoulders and dug deep inside of himself to take on his role of charmer.

As he entered the kitchen, both women rose from their table; Marian to pour herself another cup of coffee, Stefcha to carry her plate and cup to the sink. Neither one of them acknowledged his presence. He sang out a traditional Sunday greeting, "Praise be Jesus Christ!"

Marian acknowledged the greeting, "Good morning, Val." Stefcha busied herself with the dishwashing. There was an awkward moment when Val paused to contemplate his next move. Thinking about it was getting him nowhere. Action was required; he abandoned logic and veered toward emotion.

He walked over to the sink and put his arms around Stefcha's waist and bent his head to kiss the back of her neck. She whirled around and struck him with her open hand on his cheek.

"*Psia krew* is right," she shrieked, "If you want breakfast, you'd better go to your girlfriend, Elsa. There's no more free meals for you in this house."

Jeanie carried the Poppy Seed Loaf in her open palms like one of the Three Wise Men bringing gifts to the Baby Jesus. She heard her Uncle Val's voice as soon as she closed the door behind her. She tightened the grip on the loaf and started up the stairs, two at a time, to the second-floor apartment. This was a special morning. Uncle Val rarely stopped by to visit, and he was such fun.

Her mother heard her clattering up, "Quiet!" she said in Polish. She entered the living room and observed two sheepish-looking adults staring at her, inane smiles on their faces. She ran over to Uncle Val for a hug and brushed a kiss on his cheek. "I have Poppy Seed Loaf for breakfast."

He tightened his hug, "Good, I missed having breakfast this morning." She caught her mother throwing him one of her *"Cut the shit out"* grimaces. Josephine went into the kitchen to put on a pot of coffee for the poppy seed feast, leaving her to entertain Uncle Val. "Jeanie, you're my favorite niece, and when I die, I'm going to leave all my money to you." At ten years old, she wasn't interested in money, and she surely didn't want her favorite uncle to die.

After breakfast, she was told to go to her room and shut the door. "Uncle Valentine and I have business to discuss."

There was enough of a crack under the door to hear what was going on in the living room, and they weren't whispering. She got down on her hands and knees to press an ear to the crack.

"Where will you spend the night?"

"I'm moving in with Elsa."

"And is she going to feed you and keep you in the style that Stefcha's done?"

"Knock it off, Josie. I'll get a job."

"What kind of job? Singing? Bartending? Modeling clothes?" Josephine was at her best when she was belittling someone.

There was a long pause… "I can't help you, Valenti."

"Did I ask for your help?"

"Suppose something happens to you. Suppose you have to go to the hospital. Do you have any insurance? What if you die? Who's going to bury you?"

"*Psia krew!* Just tie some rotten meat around my feet and let the dogs drag me to the Delaware River!"

CHAPTER 2

FINAL MOVE

It had been over two hours since Valentine slammed the door behind him. Stefcha and Marian had gone 'visiting' to provide an opportunity for him to gather his personal belongings. Walter was left to guard the silverware under his watchful eye. Valentine had jammed into one medium-sized cardboard suitcase and two brown shopping bags the clothes and jewelry that Stefcha had bought for him over the years. He was most particular about his wing-tip shoes. He never failed to insert the wooden stretchers into them after a day's wear, no matter what condition he was in. He treasured his Oxford Spectators the way a woman might cherish a diamond necklace. These were placed in a leather carrying case with a drawstring closure. He checked the room twice to make sure that nothing of value was left behind.

Valentine's dog, Whitey, a Canadian Husky, remained on the welcome mat by the door. He refused to move when he was called to lunch. He barely stirred; he remained squatted down, lying on his belly, his head mournfully resting on his paws. Did he know his master was gone for good?

Stefcha had closed herself in her room and remained incommunicado. Walter and Marian shared a martini over lunch; it was too early for proper cocktails.

Walter picked an olive off the toothpick and voiced his personal feelings. "I can't believe that bloodsucker left. I was sure he'd be here for the duration of Mom's life. I wonder if that son-of-a-bitch has a life insurance policy on her?"

"Where would he get the money for the premiums?"

"Out of her purse, the same place he got his money for booze and cigarettes."

Marian picked up the tumbler from the coffee table, cupped it in her hands, and spoke without thinking, "I'm going to miss him, Walt."

"What?"

"Really! He was always singing and making funny stories. He made the house a happy place. And don't think Stefcha's going to get over him. Donuts to dollars, she'll have you hunting him down before three days go by."

"She might try to get me to do that, but there's no way in hell I'm going to chase him down. That son-of-a bitch was bleeding her dry."

Marian took a couple of sips of the martini and put the glass back on the table. She put her head down, tightened her lips, and kept her thoughts to herself.

CHAPTER 3

TIME AND TIDE

The Delaware River was flexing its muscles as it pushed its way north. The sun had been up for more than an hour, and it glistened on the white caps that were foaming under the gusts of a strong east wind that was rolling in at thirty miles an hour. It was the fourth of March 1943, and the docks along the Philly bank were laden with huge ships, many of which were sailing under the flag of the Merchant Marines. Under a federal wartime act, these ships hauled supplies and ammunition over dangerous waters infested with Nazi submarines to keep the armed forces supplied.

Valentine Pancross recently joined the Stevedores' Union. Except for his amateur gigs at the Slovak Club, he had no affiliations whatsoever. He was a free spirit who had no real employable skills and rarely sought a job to earn his living. He got by on his good looks and captivating personality. His previous lifestyle of creature comforts and a well-tailored wardrobe was provided for him by the wealthy widow, Stefcha Goniek.

Valentine was a gigolo.

It was a sobering Monday morning after a weekend of revelry. Valentine ordered a second cup of coffee from the lunch wagon to shake the gremlins from his head. The alpaca jacket wasn't offering much warmth, and he was trembling from the chill.

The supervisor's whistle blew; Val gulped the remains of his coffee, tossed the empty cup in the trash, and went to retrieve his wheelbarrow that had been filled by the ground crew.

"You look like a wounded hound dog!" the supervisor goaded. Val threw him a look and muttered his favorite expletive. Three cartons of government-coded merchandise nearly toppled his wheelbarrow; his reflexes were working better than his conscious awareness. He managed to center the load and did his best to move it along the rutted paving to the outgoing ship. The center front wheel of the wheelbarrow failed to catch hold of the track of the loading ramp. The track served to stabilize the overloaded wheelbarrows as they made their way up to be deposited into the ship's hold.

"Come on, Pollack, move that damn thing!"

His maneuvering had caused a minor tie-up of the procession of loaded wheelbarrows following behind him.

"*Psia krew!*"

This time, the curse was audible. The thirty-mile-an-hour wind was providing another obstacle; as he tried to push forward, the sustaining front wheel of the wheelbarrow caught outside of the track to the left. He pitted all his strength to torque it back on course in the track, but the load would not yield. He heaved to the right, lost his footing, and fell over the rail.

It took Josephine two trolleys to get to the Zawlocki house. The tall, brown wooden fence that fronted gave the impression of a mini fortress. She stretched on tiptoe to reach the bolt on the opposite side. She grunted as she struggled to slide it open.

Josephine thought the fence was an excessive bit of garnish; it neither protected nor enhanced the old frame house that was converted into two separate family dwellings.

Jeanie raced ahead, anxious to see her Aunt Lucy and cousin Stanley. Lucy Zawlocki raised seven children in the front part of the eighty-year-old house that was aptly termed "Father, Son, and Holy Ghost," - three rooms stacked one atop another in a three-story structure. The former single-family dwelling now housed two families.

Aunt Lucy answered the knock, and Cousin Stanley's greeting was a raucous stream of laughter. He was flailing his arms about eagerly, in expectation of a hug and a rare visit.

A brown linoleum rug covered the floor of the kitchen on the first floor. Four black benches straddled the long rectangular table that was protected by a brown and black check oilcloth cover. A black pot-belly stove sat on the left side of the room. It was glowing orange, throwing off some well-needed heat at a comfortable level; evidently, someone had chopped wood and filled the bucket with coal.

The smell of coffee and fried fatback, obviously the remnants of the morning's breakfast, lingered in the air. A wooden cross with the figure of the crucified Christ was centered in the arch above the staircase. A large, framed print of Our Lady of Częstochowa, the Black Madonna, hung over a brown leather couch on the opposite wall of the stove. This was Stanley's post.

Number three in the rank of siblings, Stanley, was severely handicapped with cerebral palsy. The couch was the extent of his world. It was where he slept, ate, and was bathed. Although he was able to understand language, he was non-verbal.

Stanley used gestures, facial expressions, and guttural grunts to make his needs known. He and Jeanie had no difficulty communicating with one another because Stanley spoke the language of love; he was devoid of ego. One of God's angels on earth, Stanley was here to remind us that we are not all-powerful.

Josephine's greeting to her sister was to the point: "Valenti is dead!"

Lucy blessed herself and stoically waited for more information.

"He drowned in the Delaware River!"

Lucy blessed herself again; this time, she paused to whisper a Hail Mary and a Glory Be. Stanley remained silent; a sad look replaced the huge grin.

Lucy resumed her usual demeanor, "Sit, sit," she gestured her hand toward the table. Josephine edged her way between the table and the bench and took a seat. Lucy went to the sink to put on a pot of coffee. Jeanie made her way to the couch to give Stanley a hug.

"There's no money for a burial. He didn't have a nickel to his name, and there's no insurance."

Lucy set the cups on the table and put a spoon in the sugar bowl. She put her arm around her niece's shoulder, "Come to the table, Staszek will wait for his story." She poured Jeanie's cup first.

"The city will end up burying him. It's a disgrace."

Lucy blew a cooling breath over her cup and took a careful sip. Josephine wasn't ready for coffee.

"Lucy! Do you understand me? Our brother is dead; there's no money to bury him."

"Vitzek has to be told."

"What the hell does Vitzek have to do with this?"

"Yusha, he's our brother."

"Another one without a nickel to his name." Josephine pushed her cup to the side. "Lucy, we have a problem!"

CHAPTER 4

AESOP

They were hovering outside the door, throwing anxious looks at one another. Walter shrugged his shoulders, swiped his hand under his nose, and reached down for the knob.

"Knock first!" hissed Marian.

He gave a gentle rap and opened the door. "Mom, are you okay?"

Stefcha sat in her chair by the window, a quilted shawl wrapped around her to offer protection against a cold and confusing world. She did not acknowledge his presence. His steps toward her were slowly and reverently paced. He got down on one knee at the side of her chair and reached for her hand. "Mom, are you okay?"

She turned her head to face him, "He's gone, Walter, he's gone," she met his eyes with a vanquished look, "I'll never see his face again," she shook her head to underscore the never, "he'll never sing to me again. It's my fault, Walter! If I had only waited, this last thing would have ended, and he would have been all mine again. He would still be alive. It's all my fault!"

She collapsed under the weight of her confession and gave vent to the tears that had refused to come earlier to lighten her burden of remorse and finality.

Josephine's first thought was of Stefcha. She was wealthy; she had enjoyed the pleasure of Val's company, his charm, along with all that went with his passion and expertise as a lover. Yes, she could easily provide for the funeral. A phone call wouldn't do; she would have to make the request in a face-to-face setting. She took a quick shower and changed into her navy blue house dress; there was no distracting print on the frock to detract from the austere occasion, somber and dark - that was the proper presentation. She pulled the dress over her head and settled her ample frame into it, then checked the effect in the full-length mirror that stood by the window. Her one-time size twelve was now a well-proportioned size sixteen; the added middle-aged stature suited her style and personality.

It was just after one o'clock when she set her foot out the door. Jeanie wouldn't be home for another two hours, which was plenty of time.

She was just about to cross Fifth Street when she heard someone call her name. "Yusha!" She turned her head in the direction of the voice; it was Manya, the gossip source herself.

Josephine had labeled her "Aesop," the weaver of tall tales. *Oh, well, it must have been providence; maybe Val was meant to go this way. Must not reproach her.*

"*Dzień dobry,* Manya. How's it going?"

"So, so. Where are you off to?"

"I'm on my way to Stefcha's."

"I always knew you had guts."

"What do you mean, 'guts'?"

"Stefcha's in a rage! She says that it's good riddance to that son-of-a-bitch. He's been cheating on her for years. She's sweeping him out with an old broom, and then she'll look for a new broom. She's really pissed and embarrassed."

"Well, have a good day, Manya. I'll see you later."

Josephine made a switch in her direction and crossed Fairmount Avenue to drop in at Richmond's Ice Cream Parlor and treat herself to a Coke.

She sipped the sweet caffeine through her straw and pondered the issues at hand. Social Security. *Did the man even pay into it? I'm his next of kin!* The thought was surely an epiphany. She would be on the doorstep first thing tomorrow morning. The city morgue would only keep the body two more days, then it would become a matter for the city to deal with.

CHAPTER 5

FUNDING

It took some heavy negotiating with the agent at the Social Security office, but her tenacity paid off. Josephine had always been able to make people either see it her way or give in under the weighty pressure of her words. She left the office with a check for seventy-five dollars. Not enough to cover the cost of a decent casket.

The following day, she put on her gray suit; a business-like approach was needed for this visit. She slipped her nylon-covered feet into her black Cuban heels, used only for special occasions. She pulled on her expensive kid gloves, also for special occasions only. A spray of essence of lavender, and she was off to the Slovak Social Club, where she had arranged to have a meeting with the president of the organization.

In the daylight, the club took on a dank and gloomy atmosphere. The old tables and chairs sat shrouded by chipped, cracked walls. The scene was a testament to the dramatic effect that stage lighting and alcohol had on an audience.

Josie stood there for a moment and tried to visualize the soft lights and combo music that entertained its members on a Saturday night. Valentine would walk in, and his audience would cry out, "Valenti, sing for us; sing a song for us!"

A door from the far end of the room opened, and Frank Yankovich called out to her. "Josie."

They walked toward one another. Frank extended his hand, "Josie, I'm so sorry. He was too young to die; how old was he?"

She accepted his hand and the warmth that he directed to her. "He just turned forty-three, and still full of the devil. I guess it was never in the cards that he would live to a ripe old age."

He put his arm around her, "Come into the office. Can I get you something? A cup of coffee, a glass of beer?"

"No, Frank, I'm here on business."

He held her elbow as he helped her into the chair in front of his desk and then took the seat opposite her. "What can I do for you, Josie?"

Josephine pulled at the fingers of her kid gloves to remove them and placed them neatly on her lap. She looked over the rim of her eyeglasses to make her point, "You've had years of free entertainment from this man; it's time you paid up. I can't afford his funeral. I need help."

He allowed a gentle smile to pull at his lips, "We're way ahead of you, Josie. We've collected four hundred dollars, and the club will provide the space and cost of the funeral luncheon. There'll never be another Valentine; we all miss him."

It was one of those moments in time and space when two events with a single purpose collide. Serendipity.

Out on the street, Josie allowed herself a moment to experience the feeling of relief. She had on hand four hundred and seventy-five dollars, enough for a decent funeral, and the club was picking up the tab for refreshments afterward.

Walter Goniek was on his way to lunch at the club. He tipped his hat and offered an earnest greeting. "Josie, I can't believe this! I was going to drop by to see you later today. Mom's in a terrible way, and I think you could help by visiting her. She needs to talk out some of the guilt she's feeling, and you'd do far better than the priest."

A quizzical frown crossed her brow. *Terrible way; how? Hostility or grief?*

"What's her problem?"

"She's in a bad way; she's just not rational. She's blaming herself for Val's death."

Aesop, again!

"I'm here. Is she home?"

"She hasn't left the house since Monday; she hasn't left her room."

Marian answered the doorbell, a bottle of Coca-Cola in her hand, her addiction of choice. The latest SCREEN magazine was tucked neatly under her elbow.

Marian was an attractive young woman in her late twenties, with no responsibilities and no ambition to attract some. A hired woman came to clean the house, and a laundry truck stopped by every Monday to wash, fold, and deliver the weekly soiled items. Stefcha did the cooking, and all Marian had to do was set the table and wash the dishes. This left her otherwise idle and unproductive.

"Josie, how good of you to stop by. Stefcha will be so happy to see you." She stepped aside to let Josie into the foyer, "Come on in."

"I'm not sure about that word, *'happy.'* How are you, Marian?"

They stood in the hall, engrossed with the issue at hand.

"To tell the truth, Josie, Walt, and I are concerned about Stefcha. She hasn't left her room, except to go to the bathroom. She's not eating; she hasn't bathed or gotten out of her nightgown. Walt wants to call Father York, but I know that the man terrifies her. She's been living in sin all these years. She hasn't been to confession in all that time, and now she really thinks she's responsible for Val's death."

"It was his time to go."

Marian led the way upstairs. She gave a soft rap on the door before she slid it open. "Stefcha, Josie's here to see you."

There was no reply. She sat in her chair, looking out the window. Josie made her way over to Stefcha's bed and took a seat. She was at eye level with the woman who had loved, supported, and cared for her brother. In return, Valentine had entertained and decorated her presence with his good looks and charm. Josie never suspected there was any love on his part. He was a kept man.

"Stefcha, look at me." There was no response. "Stefcha! Look at me!" She acknowledged the command. "What are you doing to yourself? You smell! When did you last bathe yourself? Have you no concern for your son and his wife, who are taking care of you and are so worried about you? What makes you so damned important in this world that you don't care about anyone else?"

Stefcha cupped her hands over her face and wailed. She made several failed attempts to speak. Marian left the room. Josie waited for her to calm down after her catharsis.

When Stefcha's sobs became intermittent, Josie approached her once more. She took her hand and cupped it in hers; she gave a soft rub to the top of her hand.

"Tell me about it, Stefcha, if you can."

"He's gone, Josie, he's gone, and I did it."

"How?"

"I chased him out."

"Why?"

"He was sleeping with another woman."

"Was there any reason for it?"

Stefcha gave a blank stare, and a confused look came Josie's way.

"Were you still sleeping with him?"

"Of course!"

"So, he didn't go to her because you denied him; it was his need for extra pleasure."

"Yes."

"Go, take a shower, put on some clean clothes. I'll pull your sheets for the laundry and ask Marian to order us some lunch. I'm hungry and I could do with a shot of vodka."

CHAPTER 6
REST IN PEACE

The weather was sunny, with temperatures in the mid-sixties. It was an unusually bright, sunny day —almost springlike, with not a cloud in the sky and no chance of rain—unusual weather for a funeral in March.

Vitzek Pancross gathered the phlegm from the back of his throat and spat it out on the pavement, ignoring a city-wide ordinance against expectorating in public. He walked up the one step that fronted the doorway of Stabetski Funeral Parlor and caught his reflection in the glass portion of the storm door. He lifted his cap and ran a hand through his hair before he set it back on his head at an angle that seemed to suit him.

After breakfast this morning, he carefully rubbed a small amount of silver polish on the buttons of his uniform jacket. Over the pocket of his jacket, the red logo of the Salvation Army announced his affiliation with the bible-based charity organization. He had carefully hung it on the hook by his bunk that morning as he bent down to get his shoes. They were in for a good spit-polish.

Vitzek's excessive grooming preparations weren't designed to honor his departed brother; rather, they were to impress the audience that he anticipated would be attending the wake.

When he opened the door, the sun shining behind him provided a natural stage lighting to project his image into the dimly lit room. Everyone's eyes turned toward him. He advanced into the room, respectfully removed the cap from his head, and deliberately assumed a military posture as he walked toward the open casket that held the body of Valentine Pancross. As he expected, his older sister, Josephine, was stationed at the foot of the casket in her role as 'greeter.'

"*Dzień dobry, Siostra.*"

She took several steps away from her post in order to distance herself. She did not respond. His lips spread to exhibit a large, toothy grin. He pulled a bright red rosary from his pocket and proceeded to the kneeler, where he made a low, respectful bow before getting down on his knees to pray the rosary.

"You don't pray the rosary at the casket," Josephine's comment was issued as a terse reprimand. "We've already said a rosary and other people will want to approach the casket."

Her delivery was loud enough and sharp enough for everyone in the room to hear.

Vitzek stood up, bowed his head obsequiously in her direction, "*Przepraszam,*"

"What's the matter, you don't know how to speak English? You can't say, '*Sorry...Excuse me?*' Just go and sit down, or better yet, leave!"

Lowering his head, Vitzek raised his eyes to look her in the face and gave her another toothy grin. Everyone in the room was riveted to the scene. He chose a small wooden folding chair in which to settle his well-padded frame, his hips lapped over the edges. He adjusted his glasses and panned the assembly, pausing to nod a greeting to those with whom he was acquainted. A few people acknowledged his effort, others looked away or pretended not to have noticed.

Baskets of flowers, from three different florists in the area surrounded the casket. Stabetski had set up an extra shelf behind the casket to accommodate the overflow of floral arrangements that towered above the handsome corpse. Valentine's lips appeared relaxed, peaceful, presenting a saint-like demeanor to his countenance. His smiles had gotten him through the rough spots in his life, but they never suggested peace or spirituality. His high cheekbones, rounded off by a strong chin, and topped with a proper widow's peak of thick dark hair, made a handsome appearance, but failed to give evidence of the roguish personality that his brown eyes reflected. Valentine's smile was in his eyes, which were now closed forever.

Josephine, Lucy and Jeanie were ushered into the limousine that was to follow the hearse. Seated up front, with the driver, was Lucy's eldest son, Ray, who was home on leave from the army. There was something about him that reflected his Uncle Valentine.

Vitzek was left standing on the curb, and since no one offered him a ride, he was left to fend for himself.

Walter drove his car behind the limousine with Stefcha seated next to him. She continued to dab at her eyes with her kerchief to soak up the non-stop tears that had plagued her during mass. Marian didn't attend the ritual of the funeral at church; she said she would join them later at the social club for refreshments after the burial.

The limousine led the funeral procession along Front Street to Richmond Street, where it made a left turn onto the neighborhood shopping district and continued its twenty-mile-an-hour crawl until it approached the wrought iron gate that arched over the Bridesburg Cemetery. It traveled up the slight incline of the main road until it dipped onto an auxiliary road that intervened between rows of gravestones to the site of the newly opened grave that would be the forever home for Valentine.

The view from the windows looked out upon a large hole prepared for the casket; lying on the ground waiting to be properly placed, was a small cement marker, a reminder of who he was:

Valentine Pancross

February 14, 1900 - March 04, 1943

The limousine pulled up to the grave. Josephine got out first and offered a hand to Lucy, who was looking at a woman standing under a tree near the grave.

"*Yusha,* who is that?"

A tall woman with a nice figure and shoulder-length, slightly curling dark hair drawn up into a pompadour, stood there waiting to observe the burial. She looked to be in her early forties. Her face had a gentle, attractive appearance and she wore no makeup. She pulled the heavy wool coat she was wearing tighter around her when she saw the women looking at her.

Josephine eyed her from top to bottom. "I'm sure that I saw her standing at the back of the church during mass," she said. "That's probably Elsa."

"Is she an acquaintance?"

"I'm sure she was very well acquainted with Valenti."

Lucy heard the familiar put-down tone in Josephine's voice and let the conversation drop.

CHAPTER 7

IN MEMORIAL

Vitzek walked the five blocks from Stabetski's Funeral Parlor to the Slovak Social Club. He had the entire reception hall to himself. The room was arranged with a collection of two small square tables paired together to make one large table. There were ten of these extensions in the reception room, all of them neatly covered with crisp white cotton tablecloths. The black curtain of the stage was closed to mark the solemnity of the occasion.

Stabetski's driver had dropped off the bouquets of flowers from the funeral parlor, and these lined up the foot of the stage. Dispersed between the tables, they added yet another somber note.

Vitzek took advantage of the situation. He hung his cap, also emblazoned with the red emblem of the Salvation Army, on the hat-rack, adjusted his jacket, and marched in the direction of the table that displayed a huge buffet.

The limousine unloaded its passengers, who waited outside the Social Club for Walter and Stefcha to arrive. Stefcha looked as though she would collapse before they got her inside. Walter took her under one arm, and Josephine grabbed onto the other arm. They supported her limp body up the flight of steps that led to the reception hall. Lucy held onto the banister with one hand and held onto Jeanie's hand as they followed behind.

"That son-of-a-bitch!"

Lucy dropped the hand she was holding and used it to bless herself, "Yusha!"

Vitzek was the only one in the room. He was sitting in the center of the table reserved for the family. There was an empty plate in front of him; he had a firm hold on the handle of a mug of beer as he nodded his head in greeting. Josephine took some quick, large strides to advance to the table and Vitzek. "Is that your second or third helping?"

This time, she used a more conversational tone, either because it was a public place or because of the solemn occasion. But none of the sting was lost.

"As a matter of fact, this is my first serving. Thank you for your interest, Josie." He fairly sang the words.

"Well, don't let me stop you from getting another helping…and while you're at it, take that mug with you because Lucy will be sitting in that chair."

"Of course, Josie. I'll just go and get myself some dessert and a cup of coffee." He sidled out of his chair, balancing plate and mug while being careful not to knock his chair over.

"*Proszę,* save a seat for me, won't you, sister?"

She grumbled under her breath, "I'll *proszę* you, you god-damn fag."

Lucy remained quietly reserved during this sibling confrontation. Walter led his mother and Marian to another table. Josephine cleared the spot for Lucy and helped her into the chair.

"You're the oldest, Lucy. This is your spot."

Lucy's oldest son sat next to his mother. Ray, whose Polish name was Ignatz, was a sergeant in the U.S. Army stationed at Fort Dix in New Jersey. He had been accepted for Officer Candidate School in Fort Benning, Georgia, and was on a short leave between posts.

Violet, Josephine's eldest daughter from her first marriage, her husband George, and their son, also named George, with the nickname of Sonny, settled into the available seats at the 'family' table. The table had seats for eight. There was one seat left.

The family table was first in line for the buffet. Sonny, six months older than Jeanie and two inches shorter, resented the fact that she was genetically his aunt.

He had an urge to torment her, so he tapped out a tune with his fork handle on her back. This was a solemn occasion, and there were a lot of respectable people in the room. She pretended not to notice, and then he used the prongs of the fork to initiate a sharp pierce. Jeanie reacted by twirling around to place a sharp blow to his stomach. He dropped his empty plate and utensils, folded his arms over his stomach, bent over, and let out a horrendous scream. Then, he let the onlookers in on the shenanigans.

"Jeanie punched me!"

Josephine, who was in the process of filling her plate, left it on the table and sprang around to come to her grandson's aide. She circled her arm around him and pulled him close to her side, "It's all right, Boobie, we'll clean this up. You go get another plate." She bent over his head and planted a kiss on his greased hair.

"You," she leveled an evil eye on her daughter, "go to the end of the line and try to be a lady!"

Frank Yankovich came up on the stage to make an announcement. "Please, ladies and gentlemen, Father York just phoned and said he was unable to attend and deliver the eulogy. So, in his absence, allow me to give honor to our beloved Val," he folded his hands in front of him and smiled broadly while he scanned the audience. "To Val's lovely family, we, the members of the social club, truly know how deep must be your grief."

He paused for a second in respect of their family's loss.

"Val was like a brother to us. Though he wasn't a Czech, his Polish blood ran very close to our own. And when he sang the ballads from the old country, from his heart, he *was* one of us. He made us laugh; he made us cry. When he came into the room, the atmosphere changed; it grew brighter, and took on a glow. After he sang one or two old songs, everyone seemed friendlier. There were tears, and members would put an arm around the one sitting next to them; it became a true brotherhood. Valentine Pancross was much loved. So much so, we had a plaque made for him."

Frank turned stage left, and a member came on stage to hand him that very item. He held it up to show it to the collected crowd. It read:

Valentine Pancross

1900 - 1943

Balladeer And Brother

Forever In Our Hearts

He handed it back to the member, who then brought it down to the floor and placed it on a small table to the left of the stage for the guests to get a closer view.

Vitzek's dish and cup were empty, as was his chair. Evidently, he chose not to listen to the presented eulogy.

CHAPTER 8

SUNDAY

By Sunday, the usual weather pattern had returned: March winds, thirty-seven degrees, and cloudy. The vigorous wind seemed to be doing its best to deter Jeanie from plodding forward after Mass. Poppy Seed Loaf would be her reward, along with a good cup of drip coffee. Her favorite chair by the living room window would cradle her comfortably while she read the funnies. The *Inquirer* had an additional booklet with episodes from THE SPIRIT, LADY LUCK, and MR. MYSTIC. That's what Sunday morning was all about.

She ran up the steps and into the kitchen, dropped the Poppy Seed Loaf on the table, and was pulling at the buttons on her coat when Josephine called from her bedroom.

"Don't change your clothes. We're going to *Ciocia* Lucy's house." She came through the hall and into the kitchen, "and be careful, don't spill anything on that dress!"

"Shit!" Jeanie loved the Zawlockis—but Sunday funnies?

They hopped on and off the two trolleys, shivering and huddling close together in an attempt to resist the blowing wind between boardings.

Aunt Lucy's husband, Stanley, was walking away from the fence. He cast an eye on the approaching visitors and turned in the opposite direction. He was a skinny, little man, totally engrossed in his own needs. His children viewed him as a non-entity.

The mystery of the genetic arrangement of DNA was an obvious cause of bewilderment to anyone with an ounce of curiosity. Where did the Zawlocki children inherit their good looks? Lucy was a gaunt-looking woman. She had no teeth. But she had beautiful, thick, dark hair that went down to her knees. This may have been her only vanity, because she kept a wooden barrel under the drainpipe outside and collected rainwater for her shampoo. She wore her hair tightly twisted into a secure bun at the nape of her neck.

Their children were tall, and only God knows why, they were well built and were blessed with lots of hair, ranging from dark to tawny brown, curly to slightly wavy. Stanley himself had a beautiful head of tawny curls.

Stanley Zawlocki hadn't worked in thirty-five years. Josephine said the only thing he knew how to do was pump out kids. They lived off charity organizations, the church, and as soon as the kids could read and write, they picked up odd jobs to help with the family finances. When they left to establish homes of their own, they continued to contribute.

It was almost noon when they arrived at Aunt Lucy's. The kitchen was warm and welcoming, with the scent of ginger and nutmeg wafting from a pot of water on the pot-belly stove. The fragrant herbs, mixed with the aroma of fresh firewood, created a pleasant atmosphere to greet the visitors after their double trolley ride.

Stanley waved and pitched about on his couch, thrilled for the company. Jeanie wasn't about to have her Sunday totally destroyed; she brought along the *Inquirer*'s special edition. She and Stanley would get to find out what sort of adventures The Spirit, Lady Luck, and Mr. Mystic were involved with.

Josephine and Lucy sat over cups of hot coffee, reviewing the events of the funeral. Jeanie listened in with half an ear to the bit of gossipy talk, most of it not worth abandoning the adventures of the fearsome threesome. Then, Josie made a declaration that was most interesting.

"I've made a full report to Frank Yankovich, along with an itemized list of how the funds were spent, since the club gave such a large donation. There were eighty-seven dollars and thirty-two cents left. Frank agreed that you, as the eldest, should have this money. So here, Ludza, take this," she counted out the bills and laid them on the table, "I suggest you use this on a good dentist; it's time you had teeth. If you need more, your kids can pitch in, they're all doing well."

Stanley chortled and waved his hands about. Lucy gave one of her sweet smiles, reached into her blouse, and pulled out a little hand-stitched cotton packet. She rolled up the money, slipped it into her pocket, and replaced it within her blouse. She blessed herself, her lips moving in silent prayer.

"*Dziękuję, Yusha,* and God bless *Pan* Yankovich."

CHAPTER 9

MEMORIAL

*"Oh, beautiful, for spacious skies,
for amber waves of grain..."*

It was Aaron Copland, Sousa Marches, Kate Smith, and *America the Beautiful* playing on all three radio networks. Every house in the neighborhood was swathed with red/white/blue in patriotic fervor for the nation's Memorial Day celebration. The Stars and Stripes hung proudly from a four-foot pole emanating patriotism over the altar of St. Joseph, in the left aisle of St. Agnes Church, to commemorate the brave men of the congregation who fought in World War I, and those who took up the gauntlet to fight in this new, cruel war of the world.

The sun was shining. The sky was a clear cerulean blue with friendly, puffy clouds changing shapes to feed the imagination. Mother Nature proudly bathed the Northeast with seventy-eight degrees, low humidity, and wind at nine miles an hour; just enough to keep the flags waving.

Josephine found the red and white cotton dress that Jeanie had shoved into a corner of her closet. She had washed, starched, and ironed it. She had it hanging on a hook next to the mirror.

There was a huge blue bow sitting atop the mirror on the dresser; that was meant for her hair.

Marchers were lining up in front of the Polish church of St. Aldabert on Almond Street in Bridesburg. The parade was due to arrive at the cemetery for the Decoration Day celebration at nine-thirty a.m. Josephine and Jeanie were boarding the El at the Fairmount Street station at eight a.m. Josephine juggled a pot of geraniums to plant on the graves of family members who had passed away many years before. Jeanie struggled with a box of pansies to honor them.

"Don't jiggle them!"

The Zawlockis were already there to pay homage to Ray, who was now a First Lieutenant, stationed in England. Joe, son number three, proudly drove the family in his Thirty-eight Ford that was elaborately decorated with red, white, and blue crepe paper. A small flag was attached to the antenna; a larger flag was strung along the grill. Stanley would have knocked himself out waving and screaming at the pageantry.

"Where's Stashek?" A note of annoyance underlined Jeanie's disappointment.

Joe hurried the response, "He's home with Helen."

The sound of the tuba and the rest of the brass ensemble heralded the entrance of the marchers into the cemetery. Valentine's grave was in the middle of the graveyard; it would be a while before the flags and marchers delivered a patriotic thrill to the observers who stood guard at their relatives' graves.

Lucy's eyes narrowed, staring at someone across the road.

"Yusha, isn't that the woman we saw here at the cemetery when Valenti was buried?"

Josephine squinted against the sun and panned the area that Lucy pointed to. "You're right, Ludja!"

She then tucked her purse under her arm, straightened her posture, and went forward on the attack. "We'll find out just who she is!"

Jeanie started after her mother. "Where do you think you're going?" Josephine challenged her.

"With you! I want to know who she is, too." Josephine relented, possibly because she thought the presence of a young girl might offer some mitigating effect against her assault on the woman's privacy.

Josephine proceeded casually, weaving in and out of the crowd instead of walking a straight line. She obviously wanted to surprise the poor woman. Surprise her, they did as Josephine pounced on her from the rear.

"Pardon me, Miss," the woman was startled, "didn't I see you at the funeral of Valentine Pancross? What's your name?"

The woman seemed to be absorbing the impact, for there was a lengthy pause while she faltered and then regained her composure. "Elsa."

"And may I ask how you knew him?"

"I've known him a long time—since he was twenty-one."

"What's your last name?"

"Bauer."

The parade had marched its way to the center of the cemetery, where a huge stone cross served as a landmark. The veteran sergeant from the VFW shouted out, "Halt!." The music came to an abrupt stop; the columns of marchers ceased their movement with a one-two step.

"Ready, Aim, Fire!" The seven-gun salute shattered the reverential silence of the occasion.

The grumbling in her stomach only served to exacerbate Jeanie's agitation. One slice of rye toast with butter for breakfast was having its way with her. Would she survive the long ride home? Would her mother ever stop babbling?

Finally, the conductor raised his baton and on the downbeat, the band sallied forth to play the opening notes of "*STARS AND STRIPES.*" People began to withdraw; the cemetery was emptying, and Jeanie pulled on her mother's skirt to get her moving.

"Where do you live?" she was still interrogating this newfound Elsa Bauer.

"On Third and Brown."

"That's not far from me; I'm on Fifth and Fairmount," she made a decisive squint and took a hold of the woman's arm, "You're coming home with me!"

Hopefully, Josephine was prepared to offer her a meal.

CHAPTER 10

BREAKING BREAD

The apartment was nice and cool. Josephine had slipped the screens in the windows and left them open while they were gone.

Their mysterious guest had gone to the bathroom to freshen up; Josephine was pulling things out of the icebox.

"Jeanie, set the table," she nodded her head toward the china closet, "use the good dishes." Elsa entered the kitchen, and Josephine left to take her turn in the bathroom for a wash-up.

There was something soft and gentle about this lady, and Jeanie felt comfortable in her presence. She gave her a smile and went to the china closet to get the plates for lunch.

"Here, let me help." Elsa pulled out the cups and saucers, and they set the table together.

Jeanie's curiosity prevailed over her shyness. She set down the three plates. Elsa held a cup in her hand to place on a saucer.

"How do you know my Uncle Valentine? My mother doesn't know you; neither does my Aunt Lucy."

She clutched the cup in both hands, hugging it as though it might be a friend that would help her to answer this direct question. She looked out the window at the huge Buttonwood tree that filled the kitchen view.

One huge splash of green was surrounded by cement walks and row homes; it must have been there since the Indians. The Buttonwood seemed to calm her; her voice was soft and low. "I was your Uncle Valentine's girlfriend."

Right on cue, Josephine came into the room. "That's enough, Dick Tracy," she pricked her ear, "children should be seen and not heard."

Jeanie measured the coffee into the basket, filled the pot with water and set it on the stove to percolate. Josie pulled out some leftovers from the icebox: some *kielbasa,* a bowl of a family favorite, grated red beets fried in fatback and thickened with cornstarch, a Corning Ware baking dish with elbow macaroni laced with butter, and a fresh loaf of rye bread. She lit the oven and popped it all in to warm.

While she was heating the leftovers, Jeanie went into the living room to keep their guest company. Elsa lit a cigarette, a Chesterfield, Uncle Val's brand. Somehow, that seemed to attach her to him. She could see them sitting together on a sofa, an ashtray between them while they enjoyed a smoke; *"two sleepy people…and too much in love to say goodnight."*

Elsa gave her a warm smile, an invitation to speak up, "Should I call you Aunt Elsa?"

"Nothing would please me more, Jeanie. I would love to have a sweet girl like you for my niece."

Josephine set the hot dishes on the table and poured the coffee, then took her seat at the head of the table. She looked over at Elsa sitting across from her, "Will you please say the blessing for us?"

"*Dziękuję bardzo…*" At the Amen, she looked up, an obvious note of nostalgia filtered her gaze. "I always enjoyed hearing Valentine say the blessing in his deep baritone."

"Did you know that Valenti spent some time in Poland?"

"Yes, he told me that he just escaped the First World War. He said his mother died, and an aunt gave him the money to return to America."

"Yes, that would be my spinster Aunt, Wera. She wound up much better off than my mother."

Josephine intentionally provided no further details, purposely turning the conversation over to Elsa.

"So, how is it that you came to meet my brother?"

It was obvious that Elsa was becoming more relaxed, more comfortable with Josephine's direct way of questioning her.

"I met him at *Zalunka's* Park, at the very first picnic in May of 1921. I went there with my best friend, Olivia, and her mother, Rose Nowicki. Your brother was called up on stage by the trio's lead musician to sing a few songs," Josephine gave her one of her affirming grins, which seemed to encourage Elsa to perk up the story. "I think he surprised everyone with his rich voice and professional style, since no one in the audience seemed to know him," she paused and looked at her hostess in a sheepish sort of way, "I am a little nervous speaking of your brother. Do you mind if I have another cigarette? I mean, here at the table?"

"No, no, go right ahead."

She dug in her purse for her cigarette case, a slender gold-leaf container that held an entire pack of cigarettes, a ribbon-thin metal band held them in place. She placed another Chesterfield between her lips and lit the end with a matching gold-leaf lighter.

"Where did you get that fancy cigarette case?" queried Josephine, ever the inquisitioner.

Elsa looked down at the case that she still held in her hand. She didn't answer right away. A sad look cast a shadow in her eyes that seemed to reflect a deeply held emotion. Her voice was soft, "A friend."

"A friend? It's for sure that the friend wasn't Valenti."

Elsa took a long drag, lifted her head, and held onto the smoke for a moment before she exhaled and went on. "He sang a couple of songs, and the crowd joined in for a sing-along. I caught his eye at one point, and he seemed to be interested in me. I couldn't quite believe it and I turned my head to look around the room in case there was someone else he was singing to but when I looked at him again, he was gazing into my eyes."

She brought the cigarette to her mouth and took another drag, but her mind wasn't on the smoke or the fact that she was sitting in a strange room with two strangers telling them a story. Instead, she was back in 1921, listening to a song being sung just for her.

CHAPTER 11

A PICNIC STORY

Bushel baskets of fruit and vegetables were lined up along the curbs of Kensington Avenue and G Streets. Pedestrians were left with a limited amount of walking space between the baskets along the curb and the shelves wrapping their way around the outer walls of the corner produce store.

Olivia Nowicki and her mother walked single file with their eyes looking down on the ground for any stray piece of produce that might have lost its place from an overloaded bin or basket. The El rumbled overhead, making it difficult for Olivia to hear her mother's comments; she shook her head and gestured to wait.

As soon as they found safe footing on the broad pavement that fronted the dress shop, Mrs. Nowicki suggested, "Why don't we stop in at Woolworth's for a bite to eat and a nice cold root beer, before we go in to look at the dresses? I'm thirsty."

The Woolworth was crowded. It was a Friday, and the warm spring weather encouraged the city people to get out of the house and do some window shopping and maybe indulge in some fun spending.

The well-known "five-and-dime" was a relatively safe place for shoppers on a limited budget. They could pick up some items they needed and even spend a dime or two on an item that might catch their eye.

The iconic large wooden barrel sat atop the right end of the lunch counter with the familiar logo of Hires Root Beer. A tall frosty glass of the frothy liquid would satisfy one's thirst for only a nickel. Add another fifteen cents and a hot-dog, with all of the fixings, would be added to the customer's pleasure. The counter was crowded; there were two empty stools when Olivia and her mother got there, but a sailor was sitting between them. He was actively involved in flirting with the attractive dark-haired waitress, who was patiently tolerating his advances in deference to her position. Signs were posted behind every counter throughout the store acknowledging the fact that:

"THE CUSTOMER IS ALWAYS RIGHT."

Olivia and her mother stood behind him, waiting for a pause in the action before interrupting the scene. The waitress looked away from her ardent suitor, obviously grateful for the interruption, "Olivia, Mrs. Nowicki, how are you both?"

The sailor twisted his stool around to check out the annoyance. Olivia beamed a smile his way, "Would you mind moving over a seat so we could sit together?"

He grabbed for his white cap on the counter and fumbled his way to switch from one stool to another. The flirting was placed on hold while the women took their seats and commenced with their greeting.

Mrs. Nowicki took a napkin from its holder and wiped away the crumbs in front of her before she sat down with her purse on her lap. Olivia responded, "We're fine, Elsa, just doing a little shopping for summer frocks." She settled down onto the stool.

"What can I get you?" Elsa asked.

"Two root beers, that's for sure," Mrs. Nowicki was most decisive on that issue. "Olivia, how about a hot dog with sauerkraut?"

Their order was placed, and Elsa took a moment to chat with her two friends at the counter. "What are you doing this weekend?"

The sailor turned his head in their direction, ears perked for the answer. Olivia responded while her mother gave the sailor a sweet smile.

"We have company tomorrow, but Sunday's the first picnic at *Zalunka's*. Why don't you come with us, Elsa?"

The sailor sat motionless, pensively awaiting the answer.

"It's been a rough week, and I have some housekeeping chores…" There was a lack of decisiveness in her tone, "Oh, your order's up." She walked over to the window to pick up the two hot dogs.

"Where's this *zoney* place?" her admirer wanted to know.

"Oh, it's outside of Philadelphia." Olivia had no thoughts of aiding and abetting this uniformed wolf.

Elsa set their plates down on the counter, "I'll think about it. I'll call to let you know, either way."

The trolley was crowded, seats were full; passengers were left to hang onto straps provided in the overhang. The windows of the tram were open, but there was no notable improvement; the weather had turned humid with ninety-one degrees and not even a breeze for relief.

Olivia and Elsa were holding on tightly to the straps and wiping their brow intermittently. Mrs. Nowicki was offered a seat by a well-mannered young man, so she was spared the ordeal of hanging onto a strap. The trolley arrived at its destination in Andalusia, and the passengers quickly lined up in a queue, anxious to leave the stifling tram and escape into the hot, humid open air.

It was a good stiff walk uphill to the entrance gate of the Polish picnic grounds, *Zalunka*/Greenery. The women were parched. Elsa unfastened the top three buttons of her blouse and swiped her sweaty handkerchief over her neck and bra-line, "I've got to have a cold drink!"

Mrs. Nowicki spied an empty table that sat beneath a huge shade tree. "Hurry, Olivia, before someone grabs it." Olivia and Elsa broke into a sprint and outran a middle-aged couple to lay claim to the property. Olivia pulled a green and white checked tablecloth from the basket she was carrying and planted it on the weathered table. She set the basket on top, in the center. They had staked their territory; shady tables were a priority. On the tables around them, baskets were laid open, dishes and utensils were being set about, kids were running around chasing one another, and the single folk were following the path to the dance floor.

Steve Leonik's Top Hat Trio, made up of base, accordion, and sax, was belting out a *Mazurka* in the gazebo-style dance hall. The sixty-square-foot structure was built after the Great War and was starting to show some cracks in the floor. Exposed to the harsh winters and humid summers, the gazebo was in need of priority maintenance. Three electric fans were busily stirring the warm humid air overhead in an attempt to offer some relief to the gyrating dancers who were showing off their spritely footwork to the lively beat of the band.

The bar was in a booth constructed close by, where conversations struck up among thirsty picnickers while they waited their turn to buy a glass or pitcher of root beer. A tall, thin young man with a crop of lengthy dark hair, some of which was falling over his eye, stood at the bar while he guzzled down a glass of the foamy liquid. He then ordered another, "…and a *pitcher* to go with it."

Someone gibed, "Hey, Fella, you gonna swallow that down too, are you?"

"Sure, if you'll come up here to join me, or can you wait 'til I spike it?" A round of titters broke out among those standing in line. "Maybe next year we'll have real beer to drink." He clutched the pitcher in his right hand and raised the mug in his left hand in a salute, "*Na zdrowia!*"

Around four o'clock, the dance floor was thinning out; stomping to Polkas and swirling to *Mazurkas* in the hot, humid afternoon had the crowd wilting under the trees, lapping up their root beer. The Top Hat Trio offered a brief interlude of American music. Olivia and Elsa did some maneuvering and were able to make it up to the front of the crowd for a front-row view. They tried to pull Mrs. Nowicki along, but she balked and gestured for them to go ahead; she'd stay on the sidelines where she might catch a breath of air.

The trio had the audience singing along to the tunes of *"St. Louis Blues"* and *"Making Whoopee,"* then Steve tapped his bow on the base and waited for attention.

"You've heard enough of our instrumentals; how about listening to a crooner?" There was sporadic applause, the audience not knowing what to expect.

The dark-haired man of the pitcher and mug incident, which took place earlier at the bar, climbed up the short stack of steps and leaped onto the stage. Steve pointed the bow in his direction.

"Valenti Pancross, God's gift to women!"

Couples swayed, arms around each other as the rich baritone voice sang the sentimental words of Hoagie Carmichael's *"Star Dust."* The applause demanded an encore, so Valentine obliged with a tender rendition of *"Let The Rest Of The World Go By."*

Midway through the song, he caught the eyes of a dark-haired young girl who seemed to be caught up in the lyrics. She was most attractive; there was something serene in her demeanor, and Val was touched. At the end of the song, he raised his hand, "I have one more song I'd like to offer to one special lady out there." He turned his back to the audience and cued Steve; the trio struck up with the introduction for *"Girl Of My Dreams."* He sang the words tenderly, his eyes never left her face:

"...For after all's said and done, there's only one girl of my dreams – it's you."

CHAPTER 12
SUNDAES

"Jeanie, go get my purse from the bureau."

What could she possibly want with her purse? They were sitting in the living room, waiting for Elsa to resume the details of her relationship with Valentine. Jeanie returned with the purse and a good deal of curiosity. Josephine dug inside and came up with two quarters.

"Here, go across the street to Richmond's and get yourself a sundae."

A Richmond sundae was three delicious scoops of ice cream - chocolate in the middle with vanilla and strawberry keeping up the sides - syrupy walnuts, crushed pineapple, cumulous clouds of whipped cream, with a cherry on top.

Jeanie was operating on automatic pilot; she held on to those two quarters tightly in her fist and was running to the door, ready to fly across Fairmount Avenue, when she heard Elsa say, "Josie, what was it like for Val when he was in Poland? What happened to him? He wouldn't talk about it, and whenever I asked about it he would grow sullen and quiet."

"Our mother was not a good woman," Josephine replied. "Our father, Albert, was gentle and kind, a very hard worker, but was no match for Olga, who battered everyone around." She turned her head to stare at Jeanie, who had come back into the room.

"What are you doing here?"

"I want to hear the Polish story, too!"

"Make up your mind, story or sundae?"

She walked over and dropped the two quarters in her mother's lap. Josephine made a tight-lipped grimace, shook her head, and put the quarters back in her purse. She looked over at Elsa, purposely ignoring Jeanie's presence.

"My parents were immigrants who worked hard and were able to buy a nice piece of land to farm in Frankford, and my father was a good farmer. My mother pinched every penny; she kept boarders, and she skimped on their meals. She left Poland with the idea that she would be going back to buy a good piece of land and live the life of a wealthy *szlachta* to show all her family and the villagers what a big *'Pani'* she had become. My sister, Lucy, was married and on her second child to Zawlocki, a dull, unambitious man, whose only dream was to inherit the piece of land that was promised to him, along with a little cabin that he and my father built on the six-acre farm. It was a dowry agreement. He would work our land for two years, after which, my father would deed two acres of the land to him."

"Aunt Lucy had a dowry, like in the fairy tales?"

"Yes, with a wicked witch in it."

Elsa lit another cigarette. "That's your sister, the one who's so poor?"

"That's the one. Before the two years were up, Olga decided they had saved enough money to make the great voyage back home. My father had every intention to live up to the agreement with Zawlocki and wrote it up in the agreement of sale. Olga went behind his back. She was always a good bargainer and had the realtor cut it out. When they came to the table for settlement, I heard there was a big scene with threats from both sides. My father had become violent and was about to attack my mother physically, but a couple of men held him down, and the realtor called for the police."

"How could your mother be so cruel?"

"You've heard about people who are fanatical about a religion? Well, the almighty dollar was god to Olga. She would sell her soul, as a matter of fact, she did." She paused at this crucial point, "Jeanie, go get me a glass of iced tea from the pitcher and add some ice cubes. Elsa would you like a glass?"

"Yes, I would," she got up from her chair, "I'll go with you Jeanie."

In the kitchen, she mumbled to Elsa, "Boy, my grandmother is worse than Josephine!" Elsa was taken aback by this child calling her mother by her first name and watched her take a few sips of iced tea from the glass she carried back to her mother.

"What about Val? How old was he, and did he want to go to Poland?"

"Oh, Elsa, he knew nothing about Poland. He was a first-generation American; he loved the nickelodeon; the funnies, playing with the dog on the farm, and he went to school to play instead of learning. He was an average twelve-year-old boy. He called Poland the Old Country."

Josephine refreshed herself with the tea and went on with the story.

"My father was told to get a certified check for his withdrawal of funds from the bank, as that would be the safest way to transfer his money from one country to another. However, my mother would never trust a piece of paper. 'What can you do with that piece of paper if nobody cashes it? We'll lose all of our money; then what will we do?' My father withdrew the funds from the bank, and my mother buried the cash in her bundles."

"Did they buy the big farm in Poland? Is it still there? Can we inherit it?" Jeanie asked.

"Your grandmother was very proud and boastful of the farm they had sold in America and the amount of money they had accumulated. So, when the relatives and neighbors gathered to welcome them that first evening, she bragged that she was cleverer than the banker who wanted to give them a piece of paper for the huge amount of money that they had accumulated in America. She showed them the pile of money that your grandfather would be taking to the bank in Kraków in the morning."

Josephine folded her hands in her lap, sucked in her lips, her eyes stared ahead, where she seemed to be gazing at something.

"He never made it to the bank," she looked over at Elsa, "there were men lying in wait for him on the road; they beat him to death and made off with the money."

CHAPTER 13

MISCKA

The villagers were in the potato fields; the farmhands were harvesting the grains, and the birds were gleaning the fallows. This was the busiest time of the year in the village of *Miscka*…the time of the harvest. The grains had to be sold at the market as soon as possible. Many of the peasants had small parcels, and they competed against one another for early market placement before the larger farms would flood the stalls and reduce the price per barrel. Whatever produce was left would be stored for the winter table. The winters were bitter, and the dwellings for both man and beast needed shoring; roofs needed thatching, and caulking was needed to plug any holes in the buildings.

The priest's carriage neared the Hebdowski's gate. The Reverend Niebojewski called out to Wera, who was bent over her potato crops, "How goes it, my child? Potato crops enough for the winter?"

"And to spare, Reverence." She walked over to the gate for a chat, grateful for the interruption.

"Where is Valenti that he is not helping you in the field?"

"He is caulking the floorboards to keep out the winter chill."

She wiped her hands on her apron and then kissed the sleeve of the priest's soutane, "Praised be *Jesús Chrystus.*"

"Forever and ever, Amen." He tilted his head to the right and offered a gratuitous smile, "I've yet to break my fast, and you are the last to receive communion, you and Valenti. Might I trouble you for a cup of tea?"

"Please, Reverence, we would be most honored." She ushered him to the porch and settled him in a rocker, "Valenti," she called out, "Bring some sausage and bread for the Father while I put the kettle on."

Wera had been a hard worker all of her life. Her two sisters, Helcha and Olga, had been fortunate enough to have received proposals from young farmers. Helcha had stayed in the village and incorporated her dowry share of the family farm along with the land that had been allocated to Olga as her dowry. Albert and Olga had farmed that piece of land until it was time to travel to America.

Helcha and her husband were delighted to buy the tract that would so nicely increase their yield. What was left of the family farm after their parents died went to Wera to plant and toil over by the sweat of her own brow.

Valenti was grateful for the break. He had spent the morning on his hands and knees filling in the baseboards that didn't quite insulate the space along the outside walls of the farmhouse. Any rest periods he might have attempted were thwarted by Wera's intuitively timed strategic invasions. "Keep that caulking going. Whatever you don't finish today, waits for you tomorrow!"

The sausage and bread, along with mustard and pickles, were set on the table. The kettle had boiled, and tea was served.

"Valenti, I see you at mass on Sunday with Wera, but I'm not sure that I have seen you at confession. Do you not sin, my son?"

Valenti held the morsel of sausage he had placed in his mouth. He shot a quick glance Wera's way and then set his gaze on the clerical collar sitting across from him. He chewed on the sausage, forced a swallow, followed by a noisy gulp to clear the way for a response.

"*Proszę,* Father," he blessed himself, "how much could I sin? I have not a moment to myself. For if I am not hoeing, I am feeding the animals or preparing the barn and the house for the winter. I am using that time in the confessional to perform my chores, or, heaven knows, I need a few moments to rest."

"He's not really skilled or handy, Father, but he has helped me to shore things up. I have promised to allow him to return to America when our work is finished. Father, there was not one *zloty* left after the robbery, and Olga, I think, starved herself to death rather than ask for help. Helcha and I have gotten the price for steerage together, and Valenti will be leaving in another week or two."

CHAPTER 14

FAMILIES

The clock on the mantle struck one.

"Are we going to eat lunch?" asked Jeanie.

"Is that all you think about - food?" Josephine rebutted.

"When I'm hungry!"

Elsa gave a chuckle at this repartee, "I'm with Jeanie. What say we go across the street and have lunch out, to celebrate our intimate morning together. I just feel so connected; my family is not as closely knit as yours. It would be my pleasure to treat and spend a little more time with you."

"Closely knit?"

"Yes, families that are connected by concern for one another are closely knit, Josephine. You care about your sister and her children. You took on the burial of Valentine, which, truly, was an amazing gesture, considering your financial situation. My family is interested in one thing only - achieving success in this new world."

"Sounds like Olga!" Jeanie blurted.

"Watch your mouth! That's your grandmother!"

"I don't care if she's the Queen of Utopia. She was a mean woman, and I don't want to be anything like her."

There were several empty tables at Richmond's. The after-church crowd had left, and the usual work-a-day lunchers were making the best of the Lord's day of rest. They grabbed a four-seater up front and ordered. Jeanie opted for a cheeseburger deluxe, with a strawberry milkshake; that would make up for the loss of the banana split. The order was in, and Josie resumed her interrogation.

"Elsa, what does your father do for a living?"

The question from nowhere startled her. For a long moment she just sat there looking at Josephine. Then, propriety inserted itself, "The Capital Furniture store on Front Street is owned by my family."

A surprised look raised Josephine's eyebrow, "Oh, I thought the owners were Jewish. How did your family come to be in that business?"

"My father and my Uncle Gustav were fortunate enough to escape Germany before the Great War. My grandfather was a minister and very spiritual. He saw the direction Europe was taking and decided to bring his family to America. My Uncle Gustav was in university studying law and balked at having to leave his home and country. He almost stayed behind, but my grandmother had a slight stroke, and he realized family was more important."

"I thought you said your family wasn't connected?"

"That was then, Josie. Now, the almighty dollar rules over the name of Bauer."

Other kids were sitting in front of the radio listening to LET'S PRETEND and THE GENE LONDON SHOW while they chomped on Tastykakes. Jeanie was in the midst of her Saturday chores, cleaning the bathroom and her bedroom.

"Don't dawdle! We're invited to lunch at Elsa's."

The little brick house sat in the middle of the row on the sunny side of Brown Street; this was the Rumanian section with St. George Orthodox Church on the corner, and the Rumanian Social Club across the street.

Josephine rang the bell and Elsa showed up almost before the ring ended. The vestibule was a welcoming entrance. There was a small table with a vase of fresh flowers and a pleasant landscape print hanging over it. A cross, without the tragic figure of the crucified Christ, hung over the enclosed doorway that opened into the living room.

Elsa beamed a smile as she took Josephine's hand and wrapped an arm around Jeanie for an affectionate hug.

"Welcome!" She led the way through a living room furnished with a modern love seat and matching club chairs. A cocktail table sat in front of the love seat playing host to a tray of cocktail glasses and a cocktail shaker. Very upscale. An 8x10 photo of Elsa and Valentine, sat on an end table. They were dressed to the nines and were as stunning as movie stars in an expensive silver frame.

Josephine took a quick appraisal, "I must say, you're doing mighty well for a waitress, Elsa."

"Oh, well, my employment status has drastically changed since my first job as a teenager. My father wanted me to gain some experience in working with the public before I took my position as clerk and bookkeeper in the family store. I've only recently returned to this house, for the last twenty years I've been living in Brewerytown where my family has another store. This house was owned by my Uncle Gustav, it belongs to my cousins now. They continue to maintain the property in the same manner, and so I live rent-free, with the responsibility of managing the house. They make their profit from the tenants who live on the upper floors."

She ushered them into the kitchen, where a sturdy chrome table with four chairs covered with gray and blue plastic seats waited for them to settle in.

"Please, sit, make yourselves comfortable."

"Platski!"

Elsa let out a titter, "No, Jeanie, that's the German version of potato pancakes, *Kartoffelpuffer.*"

"Does calling them German make them taste different?"

An indulgent smile, "No, I suppose not."

"Mind your manners." Josephine was acting blasé, like she was familiar with the German food; either she was, or she was pretending. They were introduced to sauerkraut and *bratwurst*, meatballs and a German-style salad.

"The meatballs are in lieu of *kielbasa*, and I added Jewish pickles in case you wouldn't like the salad."

Josephine offered a wry smile. "I notice you have a Bible sitting on your commode."

"Yes, I don't often make it to church services. The Lutheran Church is on Girard Avenue, which means I have to transfer on the trolleys, and on Sunday morning, after my six-day work week, I don't often have the energy."

"You know that we Polish people were discouraged from reading the Bible. The only reason I got to read it was because my mother kept a Lutheran boarder in our house. I had to sneak to read it."

Jeanie's lips pursed ever so slightly; she commiserated with the child that was her mother who was forbidden to read certain books. She was currently reading Jules Verne's classic novel, *"Around the World in Eighty Days."*

Elsa served the coffee and strudel and then pulled out her gold-plated cigarette case and lighter.

"Aunt Elsa, my Uncle Valentine gave you that cigarette case; didn't he?"

She gave that warm, sweet smile, "Yes, Jeanie, he did."

"But where did he get the money? I thought he never worked?"

"Yes, he did—when he was bootlegging."

"Uncle Valentine was a bootlegger?"

"What do you know about bootlegging?" A scoff from Josephine.

"I know about the Hoover Prohibition law!"

"It wasn't the Hoover law; it was the Volstead Act."

"Then why did they use the words 'dry' for Hoover and 'wet' for Roosevelt in 1932 when Roosevelt ran for president?"

"You little *Smarkatee*, you do know what you're talking about!"

"Josie, what led Valentine into that racket?" Elsa interrupted her guests.

"Oh, Elsa! When he got back to us from Poland, he was fourteen and floundering. He stayed with me and expected me to raise him like a son. He wouldn't go to school, so I insisted that he get a job, any job."

"The saloonkeeper, Charlie P," Josephine continued, "hired him on for fifty cents a week to bus tables during lunch, the busiest time of day. Workers from the carpet mill and the Rozanski textile mill were hungry and thirsty. Business was so good that Charlie thought a little entertainment might induce his patrons to order another beer. So he hired young Steve Leonik, a friend of Val's, to play his accordion for a paltry sum. The tunes were mostly Polish, but one day, Leonik decided to squeeze his box to a popular song by Sophie Tucker, *"One of These Days."*

"Steve called out, *'Valenti, give us a song.'* The ham in Valentine took over as he sang out the lyrics. The applause was loud, he had a great baritone voice, and Charlie P got an idea. In addition to waiting and busing tables, Val would be his singing waiter for two dollars a week."

"Was that his introduction to bootlegging?" Elsa asked.

Josie chuckled, "When the 18th Amendment became the law of the land in 1920, Charlie P was out of business. He had a lot of connections with local brewers and a couple of distilleries, so he went into another business and Valenti went along with him."

CHAPTER 15
THE NETWORK

January 6, 1920 was the Feast of the Epiphany.

The snowstorm that blew in the New Year was maintaining its ground. Travel was difficult, but Polish Catholics are a tenacious lot, and high mass at St. John Cantius was duly attended.

Downstairs, in the basement of the church, was an assembly of an entirely different nature, attended by several prominent members of the congregation. These were the movers and shakers of the Polish settlement that encompassed the neighborhoods of Frankford and Bridesburg.

Charlie Purzuczek's mother was Jewish, Esther Feinstein. She and his father, Karol, grew up as neighbors in Lublin, Poland. Esther's father was a tailor, Karol's father was a saloon keeper. Their marriage, legally endorsed at the courthouse, was not sanctioned in church or synagogue. Esther's family disowned her and sat *Shiva* for her. Karol's family considered the union a sacrilege. The compelling option for the young, abandoned couple was to emigrate to America.

When Esther and Karol arrived in Philadelphia in 1883, Karol was prepared to open a saloon in the Polish section of Bridesburg. Esther was beautiful, gentle and compassionate.

Karol was the erudite businessman. Both religions were observed in the home, where one Bible held the Old and New Testaments. Charlie was the eldest of four children, the other three were girls. The saloon became his schoolroom and workplace.

The Kaczynski butcher shop was noted for its fresh, top-of-the-line meats, the obvious cleanliness, and its pleasant service. It was the best meat shop in the city of Kraków, Poland in 1912.

Maja and Felik Kaczynski had made use of Maja's family inheritance and other monies borrowed from friends and relatives to enter the world of merchandise. Felik was a trained butcher; where else would they look?

The shop turned a profit the very first year. Friends and relatives were delighted to have their contributions returned with interest.

Most of Maja's family, formerly of the elite of Poland, had emigrated to America, where they looked forward to a thriving industrial economy. When her brother, Adrian, wrote to her about the availability of a corner property in the Frankford section of Philadelphia and offered to sponsor them, the die was cast.

They had not been blessed with children, so the transition was an easy move to tackle. First-class tickets were bought for the trip aboard the Cunard Lines.

A sturdy brick-pointed building was erected on a corner of Orthodox Street, the neighborhood shopping center. Large windows angled the corner, and the shelves inside were stocked with groceries, patent drugs, household necessities such as cleaning products and fuses, but the big draw was the top-quality meats. After the first two weeks, they had to hire additional help.

Kacper Dobrowski arrived at Ellis Island in 1892 at the age of sixteen. His uncle, Casimir, a foreman in a foundry, sponsored him to fill a spot in his crew. He needed a strong, reliable man, a man like his nephew. Kacper boarded with his uncle, saved his pennies, and remained single. By the time he had saved enough money to venture into the world of commerce, he had found the perfect woman to share his domestic life.

Lena Slota was sixteen, Kacper was twenty-two years old; nevertheless, the attraction was immediate. Lena had a strong and solid body with a demeanor to match. Dark, wavy hair and beautiful blue eyes completed the package. They were wed and immediately purchased a storefront building on Orthodox Street to set up a much-needed hardware store.

The Trawinskis arrived in America in 1878. Anna Trawinska was a herbologist of some renown in their little town of Miscka. Michael was the stable manager of a well-established manor home, where his devotion to the animals was duly rewarded by a bonus he received from the lord of the manor in the form of first-class tickets aboard the Cunard Line.

Their two-year-old son, Antoni, suffered digestive issues during the voyage, and Anna's knowledge of herbs was of no help, as there were none of the herbs that she needed available on board.

Michael was able to land a supervisory position in the stables of the Philadelphia Police Department, and Anna maintained a reputation for prescribing the right herb for the illnesses of her neighbors in Frankford.

Perhaps Antoni inherited his mother's gift of relieving painful symptoms. He attended the Pharmaceutical School of the University of Pennsylvania. His father invested in a storefront building located on the corner of Stiles and Orthodox streets in Frankford, which soon became the Trawinski Pharmacy. By 1920, Antoni's wife, Zofia, was available to maintain the cash register and serve the customers. Their three children had reached their teens and were able to fend for themselves.

Adam Stabetski apprenticed himself to a prominent funeral director in Center City, where he studied anatomy, embalming techniques, and the process of applying makeup to a cadaver.

His dream to become a physician was unattainable; there was not enough funding, and he had failed the entrance exam. However, he was gifted with the physical and behavioral attributes of the elite. He stood six feet tall with a posture that was erect, but not rigid. Perhaps some genes of past ancestry graced his birth because his family had been farmers for generations. His facial features exhibited a coolness that did not reflect emotion.

Adam's interpersonal communication skills were gracious but without warmth or camaraderie. Fortunately, his wife, Wanda, presented an empathetic and congenial attitude that helped to soothe their grieving clients.

The funeral parlor was positioned very near the cemetery in Bridesburg. Adam Stabetski was an astute businessman. Well-respected in his community, he never failed to doff his hat to the women he passed when he walked on the street.

Sergeant Michael McDermott of the Philadelphia Police Force, a first-generation Irishman, served in the 16th Precinct for more than twenty years, first as an officer on the beat, and then as sergeant. He had been assimilated into the Polish community of Frankford and Bridesburg to the extent that he could engage in friendly conversation with any of the locals, albeit in broken Polish with an Irish lilt.

Sergeant McDermott was a man who enjoyed his tankard of Guinness, and every now and again, a shot of vodka. He was fond of the Poles, and they were, in turn, very fond of him.

He and his wife of twenty-three years, Sheila, had been blessed with seven children, three girls and four boys. Two of his sons were proudly serving as officers of the Philadelphia Police Force. All of their children, by then, were grown and on their own. Michael and Sheila even had four young grandchildren to complete this happy clan.

At fifty-three years of age, Michael had put on weight, most of it during the ten years he served as sergeant at the desk of his office. He had a rugged look about him that was offset by his congenial personality. Michael McDermott was a servant of the public: efficient, loyal, and trustworthy. However, he brooked no nonsense with any of the riffraff that he inevitably encountered.

These members had gathered for this, their first meeting of many more to come to address the newly forthcoming federal law known as the Volstead Act, or more commonly as THE PROHIBITION.

CHAPTER 16
THE CONVERSION

There was a total conversion of Charley P's saloon. The bar was converted to a counter; the barstools became counter seating for meals. It was now a luncheonette that served a hearty breakfast and a working man's lunch. Bacon/ham and eggs with thick brown bread for breakfast, which started at 6:00 a.m. Soup and sandwiches, *kielbasa and pierogi* were on the menu for lunch, and *pączki (panchki)*, the ever-popular Polish donuts, were available throughout the day.

Valentine became a paying customer as his duties had been reassigned. He now earned his paycheck as a valued delivery man for Charlie P's new enterprise. He no longer rolled his own cigarettes; he proudly carried a pack of Chesterfields in his shirt pocket. He enjoyed the life of a bachelor, no longer living in his sister Josie's house. He now took his meals and bedded down in the Walczak boarding house, a few blocks from Charlie's place. A hefty toolbox sat on the passenger seat of the capacious Ford that Charlie had allocated to him to indicate his purported employment as a self-employed carpenter.

Burlington Island, a 300-acre island located in the Delaware River, between Bristol, Pennsylvania and Burlington, New Jersey, was the drop-off site for smuggled Canadian Whiskey.

The land, previously a settlement of the Lenni Lenape Indians, was believed to be the site of an ancient burial ground, which offered its own spiritual influence. Further down the shoreline, surrounded by a grove of ancient oaks and poplars, a lean-to shelter was erected of considerable width and depth. Cases of Canadian whiskey were stored in this isolated area by professional smugglers until the purchasing agent came to collect them.

Charlie kept a small boat moored on a dock in the Delaware River, a few blocks away from the luncheonette. A flexible schedule was maintained with the smuggling crew that transported the illicit liquor from Canada.

When the moon, the tide, and the gap between the routinely timed police patrols were in alliance, Valentine and Eddie Dobrowski would navigate the small craft to the island for a pick-up. The contraband whiskey was stored in the basement of an abandoned mill.

CHAPTER 17

JOSIE

One small radiator stood under a drafty window to heat the small room that housed three hospital beds. The January snowstorm had a bitter effect on patients, staff, and visitors. Josephine bundled herself in sweaters and a thick shawl to little effect. She sat in her seat at the foot of her husband's bed, shivering.

The Volstead Act had been enacted January 16, 1921 - too late. Her husband, Walek Godowski, lay there, fighting for every breath, oblivious of the cold. It had been five Fridays since Josephine stood at her post on the doorstep of Charlie P's saloon. It was of vital importance that she seize Walek's weekly pay envelope of nine dollars before he put his foot on the rail. This was her only assurance that the bills would be paid and food for the table would be available throughout the week, a challenge for any housewife … until the following Friday.

She couldn't remember a time when he wasn't coughing. When the coughing disrupted everyone's sleep, he insisted that a cot be set up in the basement to serve as his sleeping quarters so that Josie and their little girl, Violet, could sleep at night.

Walek Godowski arrived at Ellis Island in 1906, at the age of twenty-two, ready to tackle a new life in a country abounding with stories of self-made men. He had no formal education; indeed, he was illiterate, but confident that in this enterprising environment, he could not only receive an education, but he could also find his niche in a respectable career.

Godowski boarded, along with several other immigrants from Poland, in the Pancross household, which was situated close to the ammonia factory where he spent twelve hours a day, six days a week, filling vats with the nitrogen and hydrogen compound that was widely used in fertilizers and pharmaceuticals.

Josie Pancross was bright and sassy. In the four years that she was permitted to go to school, she was one of the brightest in her class; she dreamed of one day receiving the education she would need to become a lawyer. She was blessed with a strong will and a confident nature. Josie was fourteen years old when Walek, the handsome new border, arrived to break bread at the Pancross table.

She teased and flirted with him and discovered that he was a Lutheran in possession of a Bible. At St. John Cantius, the Polish Catholic Church, the scriptures were within the province and jurisdiction of the church. Although they were addressed during the Mass, parishioners were discouraged from reading the text. As it was, most of the church-goers were illiterate, or with just a meager education, unable to read the complicated text; therefore, the Bible was not the mainstay of the family in Polish homes.

The Bible became an issue for Josie. What was in the scripture that caused the church to take the stance of discouraging its congregation from availing themselves of its content? She never accepted the premise that Adam and Eve ate an apple to commit the sacrilege worthy of expulsion. Why did they scramble to clothe their nakedness? There was a lot more to the story ready to be revealed.

Josie engaged in casual conversation with Walek, and when she uncovered his handicap. She made a bargain with him. She would teach him to read and write, if he would lend her the Bible. The agreement led to a mutual attraction and then to a blossoming relationship. They were married in May of 1909.

Walek's death, in January of 1920, left her widowed with their ten-year-old daughter, Violet, to support.

CHAPTER 18
AID & ASSISTANCE

Back in 1908, two Polish lawyers and their accountant gathered enough funding and municipal aid to establish the Pilsudski Union, an enterprise designed to accommodate the Polish immigrant in the transition from their original culture and language to their adopted country's way of life.

The Union provided a Building and Loan service for Poles who wished to own their own homes; *Pro Bono* legal services for Poles who found themselves on the opposite side of the law; and tutorials in English, along with reading and writing lessons for the illiterate.

The stately two-story building sat directly across the street from the Bridesburg Cemetery.

Stabetski sat next to his driver in the limousine that followed the hearse. In the back seat, the widow Godowska sat next to her daughter, Violet.

There was not a tear in her eye. A grim set to her jaw and a cold glare in her eyes reflected her anger at the injustice of her young husband's death. A growing resolution seethed within her as she groped her way through this travesty; she would not be defeated.

At the small reception, after the funeral, Stabetski's wife, Wanda, approached her with a smile and a bow of her head.

"*Pani* Godowska, *Proszę*, I am here for you in whatever your immediate needs may be. I am affiliated with the Pilsudski Union, where you might find aid to help you in your future adjustment."

Josie offered a mechanical nod. She hadn't noticed the elderly woman standing next to her until Wanda introduced her.

"*Pani* Godowska, you may already be familiar with this fine lady, *Pani* Ludja Kristowska. She lives only a few blocks away from you, on Almond Street."

Recognition sifted through the fog in her brain. Yes, she had seen this woman at mass at St. John's, a *Babcia* type, short and round with the smile of the Blessed Mary on her lips. Her very demeanor radiated a nurturing soul.

Josie nodded, this time, a faint smile tugged at her lips. *Pani* Ludja reached for her hand and enfolded it in a tender grasp.

"I am sorry for your loss. I know what it is to lose your husband. Thank God my children were grown."

Wanda moved things along, "*Pani* Godowska…"

"Please, I am no longer a *Pani*, my husband is dead, call me Josie."

Wanda smiled warmly, "Thank you for the privilege… Josie. My purpose of introducing you to *Pani* Kristowska is to present you with someone to care for your little girl while you earn a living."

Josie gave a slight shake of her head; the fog had fully lifted. She was forced to deal with the reality of survival. She turned to embrace the woman who was about to become the bedrock of her family during the most troubled time of her life.

Kristowska's husband had died two years ago. She sold her home and moved in with her daughter. Two women in the kitchen is the bane of any household. Disagreements over the household tasks, the intervention of *Babcia* when the children needed discipline, and the alienation of the pet dog's affection led to an unpleasant atmosphere, and Ludja took to her room to avoid conflict. Spending her days in someone else's home and earning money as well was a delightful alternative for a lonely Granny. She would perform the duties of a mother; she would be the housekeeper and cook for a modest stipend.

The nameplate that sat on the desk announced the attendance of "*Pani* Godowska." The desk was one of several that sat in the legal section of Pilsudski's Union, where Josephine was now employed as an interpreter.

Josie was assigned the duty of sorting out the particular needs of a client through a screening process and follow-up with a recommendation of the appropriate service available. She was polite, amenable, and she relied on her sense of humor to engage the immigrants who found themselves with issues they were unable to deal with.

Ludja arrived every morning promptly at six-thirty to prepare coffee and breakfast while Josie and Violet got ready for the day. Once Josie closed the door behind her, both feet on the top step, she took one big breath and set one foot in front of the other with nary an ounce of angst regarding how the daily household routine would fare. *Babcia* Ludja was there for them.

CHAPTER 19

ALKI-COOKERS

The store-bought Chesterfield dangled from Valentine's taut lips as he opened the door to Dobrowski's hardware store. Before Charley P's business transition, Val was lucky to have the tobacco to fill a roll-em-yourself cigarette.

Dobrowski's was a self-help operation. Kacper wasn't about to expend any of his profits on salesclerks. Customers picked their way around the bins and counters, sometimes buying items on impulse, before carrying them to the cash register. Valentine, however, required help this day. He scanned the room until he spied his friend, Edward, Kacper's son.

He removed the cigarette from his lips, a puff of smoke emitted from his nose, "Edju, I need five alki-cookers, and five crates of screw-top bottles. I've got five new clients, two in Frankford and three in Bridesburg. Ya' wanna come with me?"

"Are you kidding? The old man would kill me!"

"Naw, he won't, he's making more money on these alki-cookers than anything else in the store, *'Residual' profit,'* he calls it. Come on!"

"Next time…let's go downstairs and get your stuff."

Valentine parked his car in the rear of the corner house on Pierce Street, a convenient location. It stood adjacent to the railroad tracks. *Pan* Janek Lipka stood by his basement door, ready to help Valentine to unload.

"*Dzień dobry, Pan.* Ready to start cooking up some mash?"

The old man nodded his head, a tired smile played on his lips. A quiet, gentle man, he had spent thirty-two years maintaining the grounds of St. John's church as the janitor. Six children were raised in that frugal household. Now, just for cooking up some alcoholic beverage and bottling it, he would double his monthly salary in only one week. Each batch of alcohol that he cooked would net him fifteen dollars.

Charley P sold the alcohol to Speakeasies in Philadelphia. What cost him sixty cents a gallon, he sold for six dollars a gallon.

Valentine and Lipka unloaded the cooker and bottles, along with the shopping bag containing the corn-mash, sugar and yeast packaged by Kaczynski's grocery store. Val demonstrated how to set up the cooker and started the mashing process. *Pan* Lipka grinned his delight, for he was about to enter a new lifestyle, one that would provide him with an income he could never have imagined. Ada, his wife, stood by and watched the entire operation, for if anything ever happened to Janek, she was prepared to take over the production.

"Valek, *proszę,* I have coffee and *pączki* on the table, come, join us."

Valentine saw no reason to object; he hadn't had breakfast, and there was a gnawing in his stomach.

After a pleasant break over coffee and mundane conversation, he thanked his host and reached for his cap. Ada put two *pączki* in a little brown paper bag, "Valenti, take, enjoy, for later."

From the kitchen window, Lipka noticed a cautionary sight, a blue-uniformed policeman hovering around the Ford; he motioned Val to view the scene.

Valentine popped one of the donuts in his mouth, grabbed the bag and ran downstairs to the basement. He emerged from the door, chewing on the donut.

"Good morning, officer. Looks like a nice day ahead!"

The cop threw a discerning glance his way.

"I've just had the pleasure of having breakfast with the Lipkas. Here," he handed the bag to him, "try one of *Pani's* famous donuts." This he offered along with a very large grin.

He kept his eye on the rearview mirror as he drove through his territory; he had four more alkie-cookers to deliver.

CHAPTER 20

MANEUVERINGS

There was a crispness in the air; the local greenery was showing off its newly subdued shades of red and gold. Halloween was the upcoming celebration; kids were preparing their made-up costumes to parade through the neighborhood. Coal trucks were pouring the fossilized ore down chutes to the basements of homes. Winter was on the way.

Josie was in the middle of an interview with a woman who brought the medical information of her recent visit to the doctor; she needed to have the results explained to her in Polish.

The office manager approached her desk.

"*Proszę,*" she politely nodded to the anxious woman, "Josie, I need to see you when you are finished with this client."

The request set off an alarm in Josie's head. She had come to love this job, serving other people made her feel valued and trusted. Had she messed up somewhere? Had she overstepped her bounds in any way? What would she do to earn her daily bread if she was fired?

She approached the office manager's desk, warily, "*Pani* Nazdek, you wanted to see me?"

"Yes, yes, Josie, have a seat," she adjusted her spectacles and reached for a file on her desk. She gave it a quick glance, Josie noted her name on the cover, her work file.

"Josie, as you know, Leon Durski, the young law student who was our court interpreter, has left his position to prepare for the Bar Exam." Josie nodded. "I've been reviewing the notes on your recent interventions with our clients who struggle with the language, and I am most impressed with your articulation and facility with English. I am recommending that you fill Leon's position. Would that suit you?"

There was an audible swallow, followed by an almost audible, "Yes!"

It was during the morning lull, between breakfast and lunch, that Officer Smythe settled his bulky body at a table for two in Charlie P's restaurant. His bulk wasn't necessarily fat—it could have been muscle. Still, he was a big man whose physical appearance alone might seem threatening.

Isaiah Smythe went by 'Izzy' as he was long ago nicknamed by his classmates in the elementary school he attended in Kensington. 'Izzy' was not a name that connoted warmth and camaraderie. Indeed, it carried the weight of a bully who not only pounded his way through the schoolyard but was also adept at threatening reprisals to anyone who might 'squeal' on him.

Maczek, the waiter, placed a mug of coffee on the table, "Good morning, Officer," he was *en guard*—this cop was new to him.

"Where's your boss?"

"Charlie's out buying supplies. Will you be having breakfast or lunch?"

"No, just the coffee. I'll come back for a meal when your boss is here."

CHAPTER 21

ROADBLOCK

The slender sliver of a moon cast a dim light over the Delaware River. A small craft, with a surprisingly quiet motor, sat bobbing at its moored site along the wharf.

Two men, who appeared to be unfamiliar with bathing and tonsorial services, sat nursing their aggravation with their choice of tobacco - one with his pipe, the other with a chaw. Both appeared rattled; what if the river patrol cops came by? There were no boats in sight, and the dull slapping of the moving current on the side of their boat increased their angst.

Valentine and Eddie sat in front of the storeroom window of the dark hardware store. Flight or fright was having its way with them. Their eyes were centered on Orthodox Street. Around midnight, two patrol cars began touring the neighborhood, slowly, observantly.

Val and Eddie had emptied their Fords. They were ready to roll; their appointed time was 2:00 am. They sat on the edge of their seats, between the devil and the deep blue sea. What the law could do to them was one thing; what Charlie P might do was another.

Worse yet, what if the smugglers decided not to wait for them and took off with ten crates of Canadian Whiskey?

"I got an idea," Val took to whispering, although no one was in the store, "we've got their rhythm pretty much tied down. As soon as the next car goes by, you run out back and drive the alley path to the wharf. I'll meet you there."

The second patrol car drove by; it was Val's cue to cut to the Ford. He drove without headlights until he came to the backroads behind the neighborhood along the river. He had it timed right; by the time he got to Delaware Avenue, the two thugs were helping Eddie pack the whiskey cartons into the car.

The Ford automobile was the perfect stow-away vehicle on the road. The floorboards in the rear were removable and gave access to an empty space below where whiskey bottles could be stored safely on a bed of straw. The trunk was a huge cavern. Ten cartons of premium liquor were securely stowed in the two cars.

Would their luck hold until they could unload the cartons?

CHAPTER 22

COURT

In the middle of the night, Jozef Blaczek sat upright in bed. He had it, he could not tolerate this any longer. The walls were rather thin in the row homes on Belgrade Street. Loud noises reverberated to the homes on the left and to the right. Jozef's next-door neighbor was on a sustained coughing spell. A good night's sleep was important. Jozef worked in the bakery; his shift started at 5:00 am.

On the side, Jozef maintained an alki-cooker. He would do the neighborly thing and take a bottle from his cache and offer it to his next door neighbor to relieve him of his plight. The coughing would cease, and he might get some sleep before the alarm went off.

He hadn't long to wait on his neighbor's step - evidently no one was getting any sleep.

"Ah, *Pani* Kowalska, I see you, too, are unable to sleep." A frown was her reply. "Here, take this bottle of medicine for Harry, give him my best."

She stood rigid, arms folded akimbo, "Harry doesn't drink alcohol. It's the Devil's juice!" She slammed the door.

Jozef shaved, brushed his teeth, combed his hair and left for the bakery; he'd start the ovens early today.

Josie skipped breakfast. There wasn't much in her closet to choose from. Her two outfits, which she alternately wore to mass on Sundays, looked limp and dowdy.

She posed in front of the full-length mirror holding a gray blouse under her chin; would this do? The black skirt was pleated; she could do without the pleats, but this was all she had to go with the blouse. Maybe one day, she would have a decent wardrobe to choose the perfect outfit for every occasion.

She had been to court several times to observe cases that involved her clients. This time was different; she would be participating in the case against Jozef Blaczek, who was arrested on the charge of illegally producing alcohol in his home.

Josie was able to meet with her client before his trial began; the entire conversation was conducted in Polish.

"Good morning, *Pan* Blaczek. My name is Josephine Godowska. I'm here to interpret for you."

"I know you, *Pani*, you are Valentine's sister. He told me about you."

Josie smiled, there was a connection here. "Please tell me what happened."

"My neighbor, the self-righteous bastard, reported me. That's what I get for trying to help another human being."

"How did he know you were cooking alcohol?"

Blaczek struck his palm against his forehead, "Stupid ass, me, I never did like the son-of-a bitch, but he was coughing one night till the rafters were shaking and I needed sleep, so I took a bottle over to his wife so he could stop coughing and I could sleep. I didn't know they were so holy and pure."

Josie nodded, and Jozef waited while she appeared to be putting together some sort of strategy.

"So, no money was involved in the transaction?"

"No, no, simply an offer to stop his coughing so I could sleep."

The trial was set at the office of the Justice of the Peace, Marek Lapinski, a former committee man who had garnered enough votes throughout the neighborhood to advance him to his new post. He was a middle-aged man of shallow principles and shaky convictions, a self-seeking opportunist.

The room was large enough to allow several benches for an audience, the desk and chair for the J.P., along with a table and chairs to accommodate the individual on trial and his defense team.

The arresting officer sat in a chair alongside the J.P.'s desk. He was young, slightly built, blonde and pale; he didn't appear old enough to be a policeman. His eyes were engaged in a self-conscious scan of the room. Whenever he glanced at Blaczek, a woeful look skimmed his face; apparently, this was the reason for his lack of focus and his general discomfort.

Lapinski rapped the gavel on his desk. "The court will come to order." He turned his head, "Officer Johnson, give us your report."

"Yes, Sir." He stood, report in hand and read the text aloud, "On the fifth of November 1923, at 3:00 pm in the afternoon a resident, Mr. Harry Kowalski, approached me in front of his home at 2013 Belgrade Street to report that his neighbor, Jozef Blaczek, was producing illegal alcohol in his home. I obtained a summons for his arrest and brought him in for questioning."

"Mr. Blaczek," Lapinski raised his hand in the air, "stand, please."

Jozef got to his feet, and Josie stood next to him. "Your Honor," Josephine addressed him in English, "if you please, Mr. Blaczek is not able to respond appropriately in English. I am here in the capacity of interpreter from the Pilsudski Union. Please allow me to interpret your remark so that he may reply?"

"Certainly," he gave a nod. "Mr. Blaczek, you are charged with illegal alcohol production in your home. How do you plead?"

Josie relayed the question verbatim. Blaczek shrugged his shoulders. He didn't know how he should plead.

Josie, in Polish, "*Pan* Blaczek, you produce small amounts of alcohol in your home for table use and to entertain friends, is this true?"

Blaczek, in broken English, "*Tak, tak,* I bake bread, I make wine!"

Josie, in Polish, "Have you ever sold a bottle of your alcohol?"

Blaczek thought for a moment. No, the only one who paid for his alcohol was Valentine, and he knew he was safe with him. "Never, may God strike me dead! I never sell a bottle of my wine. I give to friends."

Lapinski, "Mr. Blaczek, did you ever try to sell a bottle of alcohol to your neighbor, Harry Kowalski?"

Josie's verbatim translation.

Blaczek's broken English, "Poor man cough [coughs to produce an example], no sleep…late…I *give* bottle to *Pani*, make him sleep... she no want." To Josie, in Polish, "She call it Devil's juice."

Lapinski stifled a smile, "Case Dismissed!"

Josie, "Okay, you're free!"

Blaczek threw his arms up, *"Dzięki Bogum!"*

Officer Johnson stood up, a smile on his face and a warm look in his eye. Blaczek grabbed him and gave him a fatherly hug. Johnson grinned, obviously appreciating this paternal gesture.

Out on the street, Blaczek took Josie's hand and kissed it, *"Dziękuję Pani!"*

A paper note was pressed into her palm…a ten-dollar bill.

CHAPTER 23

VISITS

"…Go and may the Angel of God guide you throughout the week, in the name of the Father, the Son, and the Holy Ghost, Amen."

Sunday morning was a damp and chilly day, and Josie had an urge to visit her sister, Lucy. Since she was already dressed for church, she would ask Ludja to stay with Violet, who was just getting over a cold. After a hot breakfast of *kielbasa* and eggs with black bread and butter, she set off for an overdue visit.

The trolleys were on their Sunday schedule - slow. She stood under the protection of her umbrella and shivered. *Please, God, let there be a hot cup of coffee waiting for me.*

She gave a polite knock on the door and walked into the Zawlocki kitchen, where the scent of coffee tickled her nostrils.

"Niech będzie pochwalony Jesús Chrystus!" - *("Praised be Jesus Christ!")*

"Na wieki wieków. Amen!" - *("Forever and ever. Amen!")* came the response.

There was a fire going in the pot-belly stove. Twelve-year-old Helen was pressing her weight down on a pile of dough on the table; Lucy was wielding a washcloth over Stanley's face and hands to clear away the remains of his oatmeal breakfast.

Something had gone wrong during Stanley's birth. Lucy had been hand-scrubbing some laundry in the sink when the pain twisted in her womb. She bent over and tried not to scream. Her toddlers, Helen and Ignatz were playing with blocks on the floor. Her husband, Stanley, a man without a steady job, was stacking shelves at the grocer's for a few coins.

The family lived in a house that was divided to accommodate two dwellings. The Zawlockis' living space was the three rooms that stood one above the other in the front of the three-story building; the rest of the house had been vacant for a few months. There was no one within shouting distance to come to her aid.

She clung to the rim of the sink and felt the warm liquid run down her legs. One of the grueling pains brought her to her knees, another flattened her on the floor, and a third one separated her legs to create a passageway for a head and shoulders. Helen screamed along with her mother; her brother Ignatz's little body heaved as he wailed with fright.

Lucy was immobilized, stunned, she focused her attention on the crucifix that hung on the wall until she was capable of some rational movements. She bent over to grasp the tiny body, brought it to her chest and smacked its bottom for a yelp to proclaim life. Somehow, she made it to her knees, with the babe in her left arm, she dragged herself to the couch and waited, babe in arms until her husband came home and called the midwife.

Stanley had cerebral palsy. He was physically unable to walk, he had limited mobility with his hands, difficulty swallowing, and was unable to speak. He could gesticulate with his hands and provide audible grunts to make his needs known. However, he was not devoid of intelligence, and he understood both the Polish and English languages.

Josie pulled the scarf from her head and slipped it into her purse, removed her coat and stood by the table ready to sit down for a hot brew.

Stanley grunted and screeched, his arms flailing in the air, his lips and eyes smiling.

Lucy gave a final swipe of the cloth under his chin and Josie moved in for a hug. "Good morning, Stashek. Have you been good?" He grunted a few chuckles and smiled broadly as he nodded his head.

She turned to give her sister a hug, "Lucy, I'm sorry I haven't been here to see you, but I only have the weekends to shop and get things ready for the week."

Lucy touched her cheek, "There is no reason to apologize, you're here now, so let me enjoy you."

She looked back at her son, "Stashek, you need anything else?" A wag of his head. "Then I'll have coffee with *Ciotka.*"

Helen had the ball of dough securely stowed in a large bowl, covered and standing on a shelf over the stove. She set three mugs on the table, ready to pour the coffee.

"Hello, *Ciotka* Josie, you came too early. I'm baking muffins today for dessert."

"Dessert?"

Lucy allowed a closed-lipped Mona Lisa smile; she was toothless and self-conscious. "*Tak,* Yusha, come look." She led the way to the cupboard and opened the door to reveal the shelves stocked with groceries and staples. "Valenti visits every week to fill these shelves. Sometimes he comes with his lovely girlfriend, Elsa, who brings us apple strudel."

Josie was caught between two emotions—she was grateful for her brother's benevolence, but now her offering seemed small and trite in comparison.

She tittered, that was so like Valentine, he gave of himself, the *joie de vivre* that was at the core of his soul.

Helen poured the coffee. *"Ciotka,* can I get you a *pączki* to dunk?"

"No, thank you," she reached for her hand and gave a little squeeze, "I had a Sunday breakfast before I came here."

"How is Violet, Yusha, and how is Ludja?"

Josie crossed herself, "Thank God, Lucy, Ludja is a better mother than I am. Violet is doing fine. She's nursing a cold and that's why she's not with me."

"I have a new job," Josie continued. "I interpret for people who are taken to court. Last week, I interpreted for a man who was making alcohol in his home." She reached into her purse for the ten dollar bill, "He gave me this."

She handed it to Lucy.

"No, no, Yusha, I cannot take this. You have Violet and Ludja depending on you. You keep it!"

"What? Only Valentine can help you and I can't? Take it, Lucy, I am being well paid, and I feel God wanted you to have this. It's not so much, and it would give me pleasure."

Stanley gave a hearty wave and a screech from his perch on the couch, a gesture of final approval to seal the transaction.

CHAPTER 24

OFFICIALS

By 11:45 a.m., the textile workers were headed back to the mill after lunch, the employees from the carpet mill would be leaving in another hour. The lunch rush at Charlie's was over.

A wreath hung over the coffee urns. A nativity scene was set up in the corner near the lunch counter and branches of holly hung above the counter. There was also a wreath hanging on the door.

Sergeant Michael McDermott took off his cap when he walked through the door and tucked it under his arm. He smiled at the few customers still sitting at the tables and nodded greetings to them as he made his way to the counter. He hefted his portly frame onto the stool. Maczek placed a mug of coffee at his spot.

"Maczek, me boy, I'll be having the daily special, whatever it is, I like a surprise every now and again."

Maczek chuckled and went to the kitchen window to place the order. A dark, somber man sat on a stool in the corner. McDermott took an observant interest in the man. There seemed to be something eerie about him, as though a dark cloud of energy hovered over him.

The daily special was ham and *pierogi*. McDermott was coating his *pierogi* with sour cream while he maintained a corner of his eye on the dark man. Valentine Pancross walked through the door followed by 'Hiyas' and 'Hellos' from the diners lingering over their coffee. He grinned and patted an occasional shoulder as he walked by, *"Dzień dobry!"*

He took a seat on the empty stool next to the dark man with ever so slight a nod of his head.

McDermott indulged himself; he didn't get to see Charlie's that often. While he was ordering his *pączki*, the dark man slipped an envelope on the counter; while the sergeant made a quick dunk of the donut into his cup, Valentine covered the envelope with the palm of his hand and slipped it into his jacket pocket; the dark man rose from the stool and walked to the door.

Valentine and McDermott were the only ones left at the counter, the tables were empty. Maczek cleared away the last cup from the counter.

"Sarge, who is this guy Smythe?"

"Oh, you met our Izzy; did ya?"

"Yes, Sir, he wasn't very friendly."

"I don't know he has any friends. Watch out for that guy!"

McDermott wiped his mouth, put the napkin back on the counter, and gave a wave to Valentine. "Tell Charlie the Commissioner is maintaining an around-the-clock patrol in Frankford and Bridesburg."

Val nodded a grim smile, suggesting he caught the drift.

McDermott placed the cap on his head and made his way to the door. "Val, I'm calling an emergency meeting. The new Director of Safety, General Butler, is a zealot, out to change the police force into a battle-ready armed force."

Val drove around Stabetski's twice before he found a parking spot two blocks away. It was a dark and dismal Tuesday evening, perfect weather for a wake.

Val was much too macho to carry an umbrella. He threw his raincoat over his head to protect the Stetson that he rarely donned, as well as the snappy suit he wore to Mass on Sundays.

The viewing room was filled to capacity; out in the hall a long line of mourners queued up to sign the register. All three priests were in attendance. In the casket, surrounded by bouquets of flowers, lay the body of *Pani* Roszia Lutewska, contralto, organist, and choir director of St. John Cantius Church. She had served the church for seventeen years, never having missed a Mass that required a full choir, and there was no one in sight to take her place. The choir was on its own for her funeral Mass the next morning.

Stabetski's Funeral Parlor was a large compound. It took up most of the block on Richmond Street in Bridesburg. Adjacent to the viewing room was a reception room where light snacks and beverages were served to the mourners. A stairwell between them led to the basement, where caskets and articles of appropriate clothing were on display.

Many of the deceased had little or no attractive clothing; they were a laboring lot, content to earn their way to pay their bills and put food on the table, and not given to vanity and vogue. Most of the families held insurance policies from the Pilsudski Union to pay for burial costs.

Val stood outside the viewing room and took a quick glance at the coffin; there was no way he could take a place in the lengthy line to sign the register. He held his hat in his hand while he gestured a solemn greeting to his neighbors, who seemed to have no time constraints. He stood in place until he was sure no one was paying attention to him, then he slipped down the stairs. He was the last to arrive.

Stabetski's was the best place to hold a meeting of the organization. The members wore ties and three-piece suits, doffing their Stetsons to attend the viewing. Afterwards, they slipped downstairs to the basement, where they could safely conduct their meeting surrounded by caskets.

Charlie brought the meeting to order; "Men," was the only word necessary to capture their attention. The members were under clandestine pressure, and some of them might have activities to conduct afterwards.

"First of all, Sarge has called this meeting for an important update." He nodded his head to acknowledge McDermott's presence.

"Sarge," Charlie continued, "we'll go through our usual agenda and then you can take the floor. As of now, we are aware that the Safety Director has ordered around-the-clock patrols of the entire area, so they'll be keeping their noses to the ground. I have a copy of the report that includes the names of the cops, the numbers of the cars, and the schedule of the patrols. Patrolman Duzek is on the 8 to 4 shift, with Officer Johnson on the 4 to midnight shift. Officer Smythe is midnight to eight. According to this schedule, all alki-cookers will be delivered and picked up in the morning and early afternoon. The pick-up of smuggled whiskey will have to be timed to the routine patrolling that's been assigned to Smythe's patrol. Kaczynski, I need you to meet with me to work out a strategy for our transportation schedule."

Antoni Trawinski, the pharmacist, was treasurer, therefore all proceeds were turned over to him. He gave his report next.

"Direct sales: Kaczynski, 2,500 dollars; Dobrowski, 1,800 dollars; Trawinski, 4,200 dollars; Stabetski, 3,200 dollars; Charlie P, 60,280 dollars; Total for the month, 71,980 dollars."

Trawinski had a little side operation going. He owned stock in the local distillery, a perfectly legitimate enterprise; distilleries were able to sell their product for medicinal purposes. Trawinski, the pharmacist, had easy access to alcohol for contraband purposes. Charlie P had no problem with this. He held to a *laissez-faire* philosophy.

Each of the contributing members received ten percent of the total proceeds, minus three hundred dollars payoff money for police patrol.

Charlie, as organizer, as well as purchaser in charge of transportation and delivery, was entitled to sixty percent of the proceeds, minus six thousand dollars a month for pay-off to higher officials, along with some alcoholic beverages as gratuities.

The products used in the production of alcohol, such as the small stills, and ingredients for 'mash' sold in the different shops, were just another source of their individual legitimate profit and loss statements. There was no Income Tax deducted from the contraband alcohol that they sold.

Valentine, the chief delivery man, was next on the agenda.

"Eddie and I have collected one thousand, two hundred gallons of alcohol from the alki-cookers, and sixty cases of Canadian Whiskey from the northern smugglers. The police are tightening their grip; I had two close encounters while I was dropping off alki-cookers, and I still don't know how Eddie and I managed to pick up and transport the ten cases of Canadian Whiskey that was delivered at the wharf for the Passyunk Avenue Speakeasy. Oh, and Johnny De dropped off his payment at Charlie's the other day for two cases of whiskey and twenty gallons of alki.

The members were twitching in their seats, checking their watches for the time being spent in an uncomfortable atmosphere when McDermott took the floor.

"I know you guys are eager to get out of here, but here's the deal. The new mayor, Kendrick, took office two days ago, but in December, while he was running for office, he managed to get the okay from President Coolidge for a federal loan to fight illegal alcohol production and smuggling against prohibition and an agreement to have a Marine general take over the Police Department."

That caught their attention.

"Now this guy, Butler, has initiated a training system based on military discipline. So, we'll be using the tactics and strategy of the armed forces. Gentlemen, hold on to your hats; we're gonna go through hell!"

Charlie closed the meeting, "We will continue to receive updated schedules of police patrols to set up our pickups and deliveries."

The cloudy grayness did nothing to enhance the snow that lay in large drifts on the ghostly grounds of the cemetery. Neither did the bitter cold diminish the throng of mournful churchgoers who had enjoyed the richness of the spiritual messages that *Pani* Lutewska had woven into the tapestry of the Mass.

Charlie P's café was doing a rushing business serving up *kielbasa* and eggs along with hot coffee to the mourners after the burial.

By the time the mourners were relaxing in the warmth of a second cup of coffee, the driver of Stabetski's flower car made his appearance for breakfast. He had respectfully left the available parking spaces in front of the café to the mourners, while he deftly unloaded five cases of whiskey in Charlie's basement.

CHAPTER 25

ENTERTAINMENT

The three-story brick house in the middle of the block was a cheap investment for Gustav Bauer. It was a Sheriff sale. The former owners had left the building in sad shape, but Gustav had his resources. He had assembled a crew of craftsmen who submitted to his claim to provide them with steady employment by offering a sizable discount. Gustav was buying real estate in the northeast, and the crew was kept busy. He turned the three floors into apartments for a steady monthly income. The first-floor apartment was a gifted living space for his niece, Elsa, an added perk now that she was employed in the family furniture store as the bookkeeper and part-time sales clerk. She was within walking distance of the store.

Her relationship with Valentine was kept secret from the family for several reasons. Most of all because he wasn't German, but also because he wasn't a Lutheran.

Anther reason was a deeply felt family grievance over the Prohibition law. Gustav's sons ran a successful brewery in Brewerytown, a German settlement that sat along the Schuylkill River surrounded by rich farmland. There were twenty such breweries operating in the area, and the beer they produced was superior in quality.

The brewery was an honorable and respectable enterprise that was sacrilegiously disrupted under the hatchet of the Volstead Act. Moonshine and bootlegging were considered an abomination by the Bauers. For perhaps the only time in history, they were in alliance with the British. Sir Winston Churchill deemed prohibition, "An affront to humanity."

It was Friday night. They would double date. Eddie and his Teresa, Val and Elsa. The Ritz was showing a double feature, *"The Hunchback of Notre Dame,"* and as comedy relief, an animated cartoon, *"Koko the Clown."*

Elsa decided to meet them at the theatre. It was still too early in the evening for Val to show up at her home. His usual pattern of visiting was to slip through the alleyway that led to her back door after dark.

Val polished up his two-tone brown leather shoes and pressed his white dress shirt, donned his suit and tie, and took an admiring glance in the mirror. He dabbed his *Tous* cologne on his wrists and behind his ears, rubbed some pomade in his hair, gave it a swift comb through, and was off for an evening of fun and canoodling.

The house lights were lit as the dating pairs ambled their way down the aisle in search of four seats together, up front, if possible. Elsa was eyeing the left row of seats when she emitted a gasp... Uncle Gustav and Aunt Greta were contentedly munching on their popcorn. For a brief moment, which felt like eternity, she froze. Fright and flight!

Val was clowning his way down the aisle with his back arched and his arms dangling like a chimp. Scattered laughter erupted from the audience, and Elsa's uncle and aunt turned to see what was going on that was so amusing.

Their eyes locked. Gustav's eyes, a reflection of reprisal and condemnation. Elsa's eyes yielded vanquished submission.

Val was down for the count, a Polish Catholic Bootlegger who was a buffoon.

THE END

The list of credits was rolling, and the house lights were up bright to allow a safe exit for the audience. Uncle Gustav grabbed Elsa's arm with a strong grip, "You come with me, Elsa. I will see you safely home!" He pointedly ignored her companions.

The short drive was chilling. Uncle Gustav was seethingly silent; Aunt Gerta was exuding contempt. Elsa was shattered.

They entered her front door, Gustav holding her arm in the same tight grip, Gerta trailing behind.

"There is to be no further alliance with that idiot I found you with. You will be under our watchful eye, and should you ever see this jackass again, you will lose your home, your job, and your place in the family."

CHAPTER 26

AFTERMATH

Val stood on the theatre steps and watched the hostage scene take place. The wind was knocked out of him. He was momentarily a non-entity. *What were they doing?*

Then, rage set in. *How dare they?*

Eddie touched his elbow, "C'mon, Val, we'll go to the speakeasy and have ourselves a couple of boiler-makers."

Teresa took his hand, and they led him down the steps. He pulled away from them, "I'm going to Passyunk!"

Eddie reached for a hold on him, but Val brushed his arm away, "Let go of me, man."

His gesture was rough, hostility had a hold on him. He ran to his car, ground it in gear, put his foot on the pedal, and drove on automatic pilot; his heart and mind were involved in pain so intense as to obscure his surroundings. His hands and his feet operated the controls of the car in and out of the streets routinely traveled during liquor deliveries. He made the nine-mile drive in less than five minutes.

His favorite delivery spot was the speakeasy owned by Johnny De. Johnny had grown fond of this rakish Pollack with the congenial attitude, and Val found in Johnny someone he could open up to. Johnny was a man in his sixties who never allowed the thug in him to be displayed. He had a warm, sensitive smile and an easy conversational manner that came across as paternal, like a godfather.

Many an afternoon was spent at the table for two near Johnny's office, discussing mundane topics, recently shared jokes, and family matters.

Val never realized it, but he was carrying an open wound. At thirteen, he was transported to a foreign country among strange people who were his relatives in a backward culture devoid of any entertainment. His mother was harshly abusive. His father, a strong and capable farmer, was a gentle, rational man, protective of his children and animals. He loved his father, and the brutality of his death in Poland would never heal. Johnny was a comfort to him.

The speakeasy was tightly tucked beneath an old Victorian home. Patrons were granted access to the basement by the back door of the building, which was situated off a rarely trodden alleyway. An artful display of a green parrot was painted on the door; the color green was a logo that announced a safe haven.

The original cement floor of the foundation was left bare, allowing easy mop-ups of spilled drinks. The chair and wall-coverings were a dark shade of umber [a color long associated with sinfulness and shame.] The soft glow that permeated the area was the effect of the occasional wall sconces that surrounded the room.

Louie, the bartender, was decked out in a white waistcoat topped by a black bowtie. The piano player was clanking out *"Downhearted Blues"* and most of the patrons were singing along. Val searched the room, but he couldn't find Johnny. The bartender approached him, "What'll it be, Val?"

"Where's Johnny?"

"He's got a family thing going, you know; his grandson's birthday, I think."

"Set me up with a boiler-maker and keep 'em coming."

Why shouldn't it happen? Val was handsome, nattily dressed and obviously had money to spend on drinks. Two women approached him at the same time. Why shouldn't he entertain them both at the same time?

Several boiler-makers later, while he was still moderately coherent, the bartender asked, "Hey, Val, you wanna give us a tune or two?"

"Sssure," he slurred. He called out to the piano player, "Hey, Vincey, how about ya play *'I Cried For You'?* "

Whatever patrons were still capable of a response hummed along, and the one lady sitting next to him, still among the living, presented her amorous applause at the end of his rendition by granting him a French kiss and a gentle rub of his groin.

The capacious Ford also yielded a spacious back seat.

CHAPTER 27

ISAIAH

The streetlights shone down on deserted streets and pavements. Off in the shadows just beyond their reach sat a sole police cruiser.

Police Officer Isaiah Smythe lifted the thermos to his lips and gulped the strong coffee he had prepared for the night shift patrol of Frankford and Bridesburg. Extremely well-disciplined, he could have made it through the night on his own constitution, but the coffee added an additional benefit: comfort in a lonely, bleak situation. The only sign of life to appear during this long night of vigil was a couple of cats roaming the silent streets.

Isaiah's father was a Lutheran Minister, rigid in his religiosity; he treated his children as potential sinners, adamant that they be raised under his complete control. The God-given nature and personality that Isaiah was endowed with were never allowed to develop. Any natural attributes of creativity, compassion, and empathy had been denied him under this Spartan-like existence.

He held little regard for the undisciplined police force that employed him, full of pansy, bribe-taking officials. He held hope that this vapid environment had seen its day. A new mayor had taken office in the city of Philadelphia, and he had engaged a strong, disciplined military man to enforce the prohibition law and the crimes it generated.

However, this lack of regulation was about to end abruptly; the police force was about to be transformed into a military armed force. This suited Isaiah to a tee, and he was anxious to prove his strength and power.

Headlights approached in a zig-zag pattern. The vehicle had careened off the curb on two occasions. A drunk!

Isaiah lay in wait; the car would soon be in a position for him to strike. He threw on the headlights and yelled out, "Pull over!"

Val was startled. He automatically jammed on the brakes.

Isaiah slammed his nightstick on the driver's window and smashed the glass; Val threw his arms over his face in reaction to the onslaught.

"Get out, you son-of-a-bitch!"

Val opened the door, and scattered glass snagged him in several places. Somehow, he managed to stand up and lean against the car.

Isaiah beamed his flashlight to search out the contents of the car, "Don't move, you bastard, or it'll be the last move you make."

He walked around the front of the car and opened the passenger door. He dumped the tools from the box into the street, ran another beam across the back seat, and proceeded to the trunk. Val reacted by taking steps away from the car. Isaiah ran around the back of the car to thwart his victim's escape.

"Stop, or I'll shoot!"

Val raised his arms in surrender mode. Isaiah raised his nightstick and struck a hefty blow on Val's head. He keeled over in the street. Isaiah pelted him with the club until he had exhausted his fury. Val was in no condition to respond. Isaiah had to lift him off the street and dump him into the back seat of the patrol car.

Commotion at four o'clock on a Saturday morning was deemed sacrilegious to this quiet neighborhood where the laboring population expected to sleep in on the two days of the week when they didn't have to live by the clock. The nearby residents gathered in the street to observe the racket. Gasps of horror rang out among the crowd.

Jacub Markowski deftly made his way to the Ford the instant the patrol car pulled away. *Dzięki Bogum,* the keys were left in the ignition. Jacub, one of Valentine's alki-cookers, grabbed the keys and opened the trunk where three gallons of alcohol and two alki-cookers were ready for distribution.

Charlie P's sleep was disrupted by an urgent phone call describing the horrific scene.

The patrol car pulled up to the empty space directly in front of the station house. Isaiah jumped out of the car and deftly took two steps at a time to report to the officer in charge that he had a prisoner in the car.

"I'm gonna need some help, can you give me a couple of cops?"

The officer at the desk called out a couple of names and the trio ran down the steps to the back seat of the patrol car where a man lay bloody and inert.

"Holy shit? Is this guy alive?" the first officer to view the prisoner queried.

"I ain't touchin' this guy; he needs an ambulance!"

CHAPTER 28
EMERGENCY

At the emergency room, Val's vital signs were checked by the attending nurse, who called for a nurse's aide to wash the blood from his body and the attending physician to perform a diagnosis. She then phoned the third-floor RN to reserve a bed for him in the intensive care unit.

Josie replaced her home's telephone receiver on the cradle. Aghast, she knew exactly what the ICU was all about. For a moment, she found herself back in the chair, praying for Walek's recovery, knowing that her prayers would go unanswered.

She lifted the receiver back up. Ludja would have to come over to look after Violet. Saturdays had become a personal day off for the two women; each of them had tasks to perform in preparation for Monday and another week's work. Ludja's response was her characteristic, "I would be happy to come and take care of my little girl."

Lucy would have to come with her to the ICU; Val might not last long in his condition. There was no way to get in touch with Lucy; she would just have to grab a cab to pick her up and then proceed directly to the hospital.

The cab driver waited while Josie ran in to get Lucy. It did not wait long. Lucy threw her cloak around herself and was out the door with Josie as soon as she heard the tragic details.

A nurse was squeezing liquids into his mouth with a sponge. Val lay motionless on his back, his face was swollen, shades of black, purple, and red made an unappealing pattern around his eyes and mouth.

"What are you doing?" Josie queried.

The nurse stopped her procedure and turned to answer the question.

"I'm getting liquid into his body to prevent dehydration and to afford him some type of nourishment."

Josie nodded her head.

The hospital chaplain had already administered the last rites, and two volunteer Bushas were chanting the rosary in muffled tones. Josie lost her composure and began to cry. Lucy pulled a rosary from her pocket and, after giving the Bushas a sign of recognition, Hail Mary'd her way on to the decade that they were chanting.

Soon thereafter, the *Bushas* uttered their "Amen," kissed the cross, and bid the sisters a sympathetic goodbye. Lucy cast a penetrating eye on Josie, "Did you call Vitzek?"

"I have to speak to the nurse. I'll be right back."

Josie had ignored her sister's question. She had to wait at the counter; the nurse was conferring with two other nurses. After a minute or two, Josie was about to interrupt to make her presence known when Charlie P made his own presence known by standing next to her.

The charge nurse came to the counter. "May I help you?"

"Yes," Charlie took control, "what is the condition of your patient, Valentine Pancross?"

"Are you a relative?"

"Yes, I'm his uncle and this is his sister; now what's his condition?"

The nurse pulled his chart. "He has a severe concussion, his vital signs are compromised, he has low blood pressure, his pulse rate is low, two ribs on the left side are broken, fortunately, they are the lower ribs, so no damage was done to the heart or lung. He is receiving intensive care, and the doctor will be visiting him frequently. We will do everything necessary to keep him alive."

"I'll kill the bastard!" Charlie muttered under his breath,

"Thank you, Nurse." Josie offered a grateful smile to offset Charlie's remark.

They walked back to Val's room. Lucy was still at prayer with her beads. Charley bent to kiss her head, "He's got to pull through with an angel like you praying for him."

He took a long look at his friend. Val had been a good trafficker, and one hell of a guy.

"Ladies, I have to go. I have a busy day ahead of me." He took one last look at Val, "God Bless all of you."

Charlie P drove to the wharf, picked up five cases of whiskey, delivered them to the vacant mill where the alcohol was stored and was back for his breakfast at the restaurant before eight o'clock that morning.

He went to his office, checked his receipts and the delivery log, and made a phone call to Dobrowski's.

"Kacper, that bastard cop, Smythe beat the shit out of Val; he's in the hospital, I need Eddy to take over the transporting routes."

CHAPTER 29

DISAPPEARANCE

Eddie was not in his room. It was after nine before he finally came home; he had spent the night with Teresa.

"Where the hell were you all night? Keep this up and you'll find yourself in one hell of a mess!"

Eddie held his temper in check; who the hell did the old man think he was talking to, a twelve-year-old? He let it roll by with a smirk and a roll of his eyes.

"Val's in the hospital. You'll have to pick up his alki route. Get over to Charlie's and pick up the list. NOW!"

"What do you mean, Val's in the hospital? What for?"

"That idiot Izzy beat the shit out of him."

"I'm going to the hospital!" He turned to walk out the door.

"You do and you'll have Charlie to answer to. Val's unconscious, he won't even know you're there. Get going. You'll see him after you finish the rounds."

"I'm gonna call Elsa, first!"

The phone rang, but there was no answer; he'd call her from Charlie's place.

His last delivery was to Passyunk Avenue. Johnny De was sitting at his table in the corner of the room, going over his receipts from Friday night.

"Hi, Johnny."

"Ed, my boy; are you alone? Where's Val?"

"He's in the hospital; that cop, Izzy, beat him up. He's unconscious."

His posture became rigid. He stared ahead while he digested this nasty bit of information. He brought his fist to his face, stuck out his thumb, and flicked it under his chin. A Mafioso gesture that implies revenge.

Elsa didn't answer her phone when Eddie tried again to call her from Charlie's. Perhaps that was a good thing; better to give such dire news face-to-face.

Eddie was finished for the day, so he figured he would drop by her house and offer her emotional support.

She didn't answer his knock on the door. He was confused and frustrated when luck offered him an informant. The tenant from the second floor was returning home with a package from the local deli.

"Hi, do you know where Elsa is?"

"Oh, yeah, her uncle stopped by and took her to Brewerytown. The family's opening a new store there. Her uncle left me in charge of the house."

"Did she leave a number where she could be reached?"

"No, I'm to call the furniture store on Front Street if anything happens."

CHAPTER 30

REPERCUSSIONS

Sergeant Michael McDermott hung his cap on the peg, unbuttoned his heavy woolen jacket, hung it on the rack, and made for the men's room. Cold weather had a stimulating effect on his bladder.

He clocked in and then checked the duty roster with the officers ready to begin their shift. On his way to the desk, he grabbed a hot cup of coffee to start his day right. He sat down at his desk to check the night's report. He hadn't finished the first report when he had to pause - he felt his stress level rising. He lay the page on his desk, stared ahead, and pursed his lips. He sat there a moment to contemplate - to digest the report from Officer Smythe. He picked up the phone and dialed the hospital's number.

After receiving the diagnostic assessment of Valentine Pancross, he sat back in his chair, his emotions grinding him into action. He picked up the phone and dialed Isaiah Smythe's number. "Get your ass in her pronto!"

Sergeant McDermott was well respected by his men; he was fair and sensible, not one to rule by the "my way or the highway" method. He was once a rookie himself. He had made mistakes, and he would judiciously work out any minor infractions an officer in his ranks might perform in his line of duty. But Isaiah Smythe had crossed the line.

Smythe was not at all happy to be woken from his sleep after a bitter cold night's duty and the rumble he had with a drunk he arrested in the middle of the night. When he heard the arrogant, hostile tone in the command his Sergeant imposed on him, his belligerent nature rose to the occasion.

Who the hell does he think he is? I'll get there when I'm goddamned good and ready.

McDermott peered at him over his glasses, then he removed the spectacles slowly. "You took your goddamned time."

Smythe walked over to the desk. "You have a problem?"

"No, Officer Smythe, you have a problem!" He banged his fist on the desk, "What the hell kind of a human being are you? Don't answer, I don't think you have an answer. You're a goddamned Neanderthal. What do you mean, beating a man to death? Where the hell did you read in the manual that such an act would be condoned? I sent a report of the incident to Lieutenant Porter. You're suspended for ten days until we figure out what the hell to do with you. Now get the hell out of my sight before I pick up *my* nightstick."

CHAPTER 31

JUSTICE

Philadelphia City Hall, a massive structure of brick, marble, and limestone, majestically holds court of an entire city block in the busy downtown shopping area. It was as though the bustling traffic gradually developed to surround this government complex. It was considered to be the world's largest free-standing building, and also the tallest. The groundbreaking ceremony took place in 1871. It was completed and opened for business in 1901. The statue of William Penn sits atop the tower, maintaining a discerning eye over his *'City of Brotherly Love'*. A city planning law was carved in stone; no future building could be erected to surpass the height of Billy Penn's hat.

January 1924: the council meeting got a late start, as it usually did. Seven o'clock in the evening was an inconvenient time for members and audience alike to commit to. There was dinner and freshening up after a day's work to attend to, and the leftover snow was another issue to deal with. However, an unprecedented crowd filled the large room. The new Director of Public Safety was being introduced to the city.

First on the agenda was the reorganization of the police force under Marine Corps General Smedley Darlington Butler.

He had gained the audience's attention before the gavel was struck. A handsome man in the crisp military uniform of the Marines, he was tall and lean, an athletic sort, his face was long and thin, and his short-cut hair was graying. His posture was statuesque. The mayor introduced him, throwing kudos his way.

"Good evening, Mayor Kendrick, Councilmen, and citizens of Philadelphia," his baritone voice carried without a microphone; his articulation was precise, all the elements of a practiced speech maker.

"Since the passing of the Volstead Act, America has been at war, and frankly, the mighty government is losing the battle to the criminals involved in the lucrative business of bootlegging. Your honorable mayor has appealed to President Coolidge for someone to take command of the Philadelphia Police Force and whip them into a successful fighting force. I have received that commission."

The speech was interrupted by a gusty applause from the audience. The general accepted the praise with a nod of his head, waiting for the din to end so he could resume his speech. "Before we address the strategies to be employed, it is necessary to begin with the root of the problem - the wages paid to the men who daily risk their lives by providing security to the citizens of this great city. The average mill worker earns approximately one thousand four hundred dollars a year, whereas the average policeman earns one thousand three hundred dollars a year." Audience members looked at one another in surprise at the relevant comparison.

"The first thing we must do is raise the salary of our men in uniform. In tandem with that resolution, I will begin a training operation for our men to fight with effective tactics." He turned his head in the direction of the mayor, "Mayor Kendrick, do I have your support in this matter?"

"Your request will be a priority issue on the city planning agenda. We will use the Federal Aid allotted to us for enforcement and somehow come up with a special fund for the purpose."

Cases of minor infractions were within the bailiwick of Lieutenant Arnold Porter, General Butler's aide. During his twenty-four-year career of dealing with thugs and their families, Porter was able to make an accurate measure of a man. He could size up a phony and appreciate the honesty of a man. As Lieutenant, he conducted the hearings brought before him in a rational and logical manner. He opened the file on his desk, a brutality case against a police officer.

Isaiah Smythe skipped breakfast this Tuesday morning; he didn't want to put himself out with the possibility of using the unsanitary conditions of a public bathroom. He packed his portly body behind the wheel of his Model T and deftly drove through the busy early morning traffic. Cursed by his obsession with punctuality, he arrived at the entrance of City Hall at 8:45 a.m. The door would not open until for another fifteen minutes at 9:00 a.m.

Frigid cold pierced through the solid masonry walls of the gigantic building. The roaring fires in the basement furnaces had not yet accomplished their directive. In the office of Lieutenant Porter, a clerk set the percolator going for coffee to offset the chill and offer a more congenial atmosphere. Porter sat down at his desk, removed his hat but not his anorak. He laid the file of Officer Isaiah Smythe open before him.

Sergeant McDermott sat next to him, hat removed, wrapped in his anorak with Officer Isaiah Smythe's file unopened beneath his left hand. On the other side of the desk, Officer Smythe sat huddled in his overcoat, holding a clipboard of notes. The clerk brought three large mugs of steaming coffee, and a mundane conversation regarding the weather made a brief appearance before they got down to the issue at hand.

The clerk sat at a small table, stenographer's book and pen in hand to take notes.

Lieutenant Porter, "We are here to settle a public brutality case, a civil rights violation, against Officer Isaiah Smythe. The outcome of this case will determine the continued employment of Officer Smythe." He reached for the Gideon Bible on his left and placed it at the right hand of Isaiah, "Officer Isaiah Smythe, do you promise to tell the truth, the whole truth, and nothing but the truth, so help you God?"

Isaiah's face mirrored the climate of the room, grimly dispassionate, "I do."

Porter commanded, "Go ahead. Give your report."

Smythe ahemed his way to his feet, "At approximately 4:00 a.m. 11 January, an auto careened off the curb of pavement on Margaret Street, driven by a man influenced by alcohol. I pulled the vehicle to the side and asked the driver to step out of his car, which he did. When I asked for his license, he reached for his wallet, but then he turned around and swung at me, hitting me on the jaw. I grabbed him by the collar, and that's when he kicked me in the groin. I reacted to the pain by swinging my nightstick at him hard on the head. He fell to the ground. I tried to get him to stand up, but he was unconscious. Somehow, I managed to get him into the back of the patrol car and drove to the police station. He remained unconscious and was taken to the hospital. The man was clearly resisting arrest. Sergeant McDermott sent an incident report, and I was accused of brutality when, clearly, I was merely defending myself. I was given a ten-day suspension for doing my job."

Porter, "Sergeant McDermott, will you read your report of the incident?"

McDermott looked at his watch, 9:17, perfect timing, the hospital report would give him the extra minutes he needed for his anticipated disruption of the proceedings.

"I have here two affidavits signed by the officers on duty the morning of 11 January 1924. They are accurate descriptions of the condition of one Valentine Pancross, a subject brought in under arrest by Officer Isaiah Smythe."

McDermott placed the documents on the desk for perusal. A knock on the door interrupted his report. The door opened to a tall, well-built young man who stood in the doorway while he politely ushered in a middle-aged woman bundled to the ears with a wool *Babushka* and a heavy scarf.

"Excuse us, we are late for this hearing, my car wouldn't start in this cold. I apologize!"

Porter shot a glance over at McDermott, and Isaiah threw a look at the intruder. McDermott rose from his chair to welcome his star witnesses.

"Lieutenant, may I present the eye-witnesses of the scene that took place on Margaret Street the morning of 11 January. These are witnesses who were woken from their beds during the harassment, Mr. Jacub Markowski and Mrs. Irene Gouda."

Porter checked for any emotion on Smythe's face… incredulous shock registered on his stony countenance.

"Good morning, I am Lieutenant Porter, officiating the case against Officer Isaiah Smythe."

The raising of the right hand over the bible and the commitment, "I do," were duly noted.

"Mr. Markowski, will you begin your testimony?"

"Yes, Sir, it was about four in the morning on a Saturday, when working people could sleep in, a police siren screeched under my window. I looked out and saw the police car and a Ford. The cop got out of his vehicle and walked toward the Ford. I got into my robe and slippers and ran downstairs to see what was going on. By the time I got out the door, the cop smashed the driver's side window with his nightstick. He yelled at the driver to get out of his car. The poor guy must have gotten cut up by the broken glass, but he got out and stood next to his car. The cop ordered him to stay where he was while he ran around the Ford to check on the seats. He came back to the guy and started bashing him with his nightstick. The poor devil fell down on the street, and the cop started kicking him. No way could that guy stand up to get into the patrol car. The cop was a big, strong guy, but I don't know how he got him into the back seat; the guy was dead weight."

The clerk's pen picked up the rhythm of the witness's tale for future reference.

Markowski took a seat on the bench that stood by the door while the next witness gave her testimony.

"Mrs. Gouda, will you tell us what you saw during the arrest of the subject?"

"Yes, Your Honor. I didn't go out in the street when I heard the siren, but people were screaming, and I was frightened. I put on my coat and went to find out what was happening. My neighbor, Sophie, was crying. I looked out in the street and saw a man standing next to his car. A cop was beating this man with a stick. I thought he beat him to death because the man fell to the ground and didn't move. The cop picked him up and threw him in the back seat. All of us stood there cursing the cop and praying the man would live."

"Mr. Markowski," Porter asked the first witness, "at any time, during this incident, did you see the man striking back?"

"No, Sir, he never got a chance. He was hurting from the time he got out of his car."

"Mrs. Gouda," Porter repeated the question to the woman, "at any time, during this incident, did you see the man striking back?"

"No, Your Honor," a crack in her voice, "he had no fight in him, he was beaten until he fell into the street." She broke down in tears.

CHAPTER 32

REDEMPTION

It was 7:37 a.m. The sun was rising on Wednesday morning, the fourteenth of February. Valentine Pancross twitched in the bed; his mouth was dry. He felt numb inside and a vague notion gnawed at him with the perplexing question of his whereabouts and identity. He opened his eyes. There was a familiarity about the green room he was in. The white door stood in the corner of the wall facing him…but he had no idea where this room was situated.

The door opened and a nurse entered the room carrying a bowl and sponge. She reacted, ever so startled, "Oh, my God?"

His blood pressure was low, his heart rate steady, dehydration was a major factor, and, of course, nourishment. He was placed on a liquid diet that was to commence immediately.

The nurse addressed him as "Mr. Pancross," and for a moment that held no meaning for him, and then his first name raced to his conscious awareness, 'Valentine'. His emotional engine remained idling; homeostasis was juggling his physical composition as a major priority.

A huge red cardboard heart hung from the cornice over the counter. A bowl of red roses took center stage on the counter, next to Charlie P's *kielbasa* and eggs. The first rays of sunlight were beaming through the windows of the café during the morning rush, and Charlie had an announcement to make; he turned around on the stool and faced his weary patrons.

"Valentine woke up yesterday!" Smiles lit their faces', and a general applause rang out, along with shouts of *"Dzięki Bogum!"*

"I stopped by yesterday, to see how he was doing. He's still weak and he seemed a bit confused," a chuckle, "but that's not unusual for him." He waited while the laughter subsided. "That son-of-a-bitch, Izzy got what he deserved; he's cooling his heels in a prison cell for perjury. We won't be seeing his face for the next year!"

The sun beamed brightly over the path of the mill workers as they made their routine walk to the mill to start another twelve-hour shift. A hearty breakfast, along with a general opinion that God's justice had prevailed would see them through the day.

Victor, the hospital orderly, was aptly named. He stood over six feet tall and had the build of a football fullback. He had a no-nonsense approach to his varied duties, which included sponge baths. He entered the room pushing a little cart before him. A basin, sponge, a bar of soap, washcloths, and towels were neatly arranged on its shelves.

"Good morning, Mister Pancross. I'm Victor, and I'm here to get you ready for the day."

"Good morning, Victor, please, my name is Valentine. Mister Pancross was my father." A large smile lit his eyes.

"I see that you are still on bedpan and urinal. Have you been out of bed at all?"

"Not yet."

"Then the first thing we have to do is get you to stand up." He moved close to the bed and offered his shoulder and arm for support. Val put his arm on the available shoulder and grabbed a tight hold on Victor's hand. He wobbled to a standing position and was surprised to find his legs would not hold him.

"Lean on me; it's going to take a while before your legs remember what they're supposed to do."

He took a firm hold around Val's waist, "Okay, Mister Pancross, try to take a few steps."

The sponge bath was completed, he was shaved, and a comb was raked across his long hair to settle behind his ears. He was clad in a clean gown and offered a robe and slippers. Mister Pancross felt respectfully human.

Victor provided a wheelchair and drove him to the hall. Valentine was free to roam.

It was around ten-thirty, an hour and a half until lunch. He wound his way to the solarium; a huge plate-glass window looked out on the world Val had not seen since his brutal beating.

The view was commonplace: a few leafless trees recently adorned with snow, and a row of three-story brick homes, a scene that nonetheless brought excitement to his soul. He crossed himself with gratitude and whispered, *"Dzięki Bogum!"*

Just before noon, the Nurse's Aide, Patricia, wheeled the medicine cart into the solarium. "Good morning, Mister Pancross." After his encounter with Victor, he made no effort to offer a less formal atmosphere by providing his first name.

"Good morning."

Patricia filled a tiny soufflé cup with the proper dosage of Val's prescriptions, filled a glass of water and served her patient. Val took the cup from her hand and turned her palm down, "You have lovely hands, Nurse," he looked up into her green eyes, "Most people judge another's personality by looking in the eyes; I go by what I see in a person's hands. Men with big hands and rough fingernails are heavy laborers, men and women with long fingers are artists, women with big hands are in command of their lives, and people with small hands, like yours, are soft and gentle."

Nurse Patricia was also blessed with an abundance of auburn hair and thick lashes that drew attention to her green eyes; her lips, though thin, were delightfully expressive. The starched uniform and crisp apron could not conceal the petite, neatly formed figure beneath.

She grew anxious as the situation was embarrassing; she withdrew her hand.

"Thank you, Mister Pancross, now if you would just take your pills."

Val looked directly into her eyes, a rueful smile gave way to a sincere apology, which Nurse Patricia acknowledged by returning the smile.

He nodded politely, and wondered how long it would take to have Nurse Patricia call him Val.

Now that he had a set of wheels beneath him, Val took to exploring his current living arrangements, he romanced the charge nurse, shared his beer pretzels with the janitor, and toured the X-Ray department.

By seven o'clock, he was ready for visitors.

Charlie and Eddie arrived together. Val ushered them into the solarium.

"We didn't bring you anything to drink because it might not be good for you," Charlie handed him a small cardboard box, "Here's some *chruszicki* for you to munch on."

"Hey, *Dziękuję bardzo!*"

He looked directly at Eddie, "How's Elsa? Why hasn't she been here to see me?"

Eddie faced the issue directly, "She's in Brewerytown with her uncle; he's opened a new store. I can't get a hold of her because I can't get the number to the store."

Val stared blankly, after an exaggerated pause, "Charlie, get me out of here; I gotta find her!"

"Whoa, there fella. I got no control over your stay in the hospital; you need to talk to your doctor about that."

Val called out, "Nurse!"

"Calm down, Val, you're making an ass of yourself."

"Go to hell, Charlie," he shouted again, "Nurse!"

The charge nurse rushed in, "What is it, Mister Pancross?"

"Nurse, I gotta get out of here. Phone the doctor, I want out of here!"

CHAPTER 33

RESILIENCE

Charlie P showed up at the registration desk precisely at ten a.m. to pay Val's bill and accept his prescriptions. He presented Val with a sturdy cane to support his weakened legs and helped him into the front seat of his Cadillac.

The first stop was Brown Street. Val hobbled to the doorstep and rang the bell. A dark-haired, stout woman opened the door. Val could see the familiar furnishings of the living room. "I need to see Elsa."

"Elsa Bauer?" She queried with a Rumanian accent.

"Yes."

"She lives in Brewerytown."

"What's her address? What's her phone number?"

She addressed the question with a sarcastic tone, "I don't know!"

Her reply irked him; he was unsettled in his emotions to begin with, and her attitude added fuel to the fire. "Who are you?"

His tone evoked a much more submissive demeanor, "My husband is caretaker of church. We know nothing about Elsa Bauer, we rent from Mr. Bauer at store."

Charlie wasn't up to it, but Val was insistent, and considering his fragile condition, Charlie acquiesced.

This time, Charlie accompanied him; no telling what effect the encounter would have on Val.

They walked past the solicitous salesman and went to the office where Elsa's cousin Nina sat in charge.

"Where's Elsa?"

"Good morning, Valentine," she looked down at the cane he wielded, "What happened to you? Were you in an accident?"

"Where's Elsa Bauer?"

"You mean Elsa Memming. She's happily married to a wealthy manufacturer," a smirk revealed the contempt she had regarding his past affiliation with a member of her family, "so you see, I cannot give you that information, nor should you want to know how happy she is in her new life."

Val rested his forehead on his left hand, his legs were unsteady. He was unable to absorb the impact of her words, Charlie grabbed a hold on him before he collapsed.

"You son-of-a-heartless-bitch!"

Val made an effort to appear pleased with the attention the diners were throwing at him.

Charlie himself brought the bowl of *gołąbki* to the table, "Here ya go, fella, you haven't had a meal like this since Izzy beat the shit out of you. You know he's doing a year in prison for perjury, don't you?"

That brought a smile to Val's face, and when the rest of the folk in the dining room saw this, applause rang out. The smile remained on his face, and he poked his fork and knife into his bowl of *gołąbki.*

The café was closed for the day, Charlie and Val remained at the table.

"Maczek, bring us a bottle of vodka and a couple of glasses."

Charlie poured and raised his glass, *"Na Zdrowia!"*

Val nodded his head, *"Na Zdrowia!"*

"Okay, Val, this is the deal. I got big plans for you. Butler is making things tough; he's got some loyal cops under him, and so far he's closed over five hundred speakeasies…"

Val interrupted, "Did he get Johnny De's?"

"Yeah, Johnny lost his brand of loyal officers. Butler's military strategy can't be beat. He switched patrol units to different locations all over the city; we got the unit from Chestnut Hill.

"But here's the thing. We've lost sixty so far, but we still have that cadre of rich guys who are paying the increased rate, so I got plans to keep them supplied with Canadian. In the meantime, you have to recuperate. I'm making you busboy and janitor of the café until you're on your feet again."

CHAPTER 34

PLANS

Early Saturday morning, Josie and Violet stood on the front step of the Walczak boarding house. Bundled in their jackets and scarves, they were armed with cleaning supplies, a dustpan and brush, polishing cloth, and a bar of lye soap filled the bucket that Josie carried, while Violet held on to the mop like a staff. Josie rang the doorbell.

The housekeeper opened the door, "Irma, good morning, we're here to clean Valentine's room before he comes home." Josie pushed her way into the foyer with Violet behind her.

"*Pani*, there is no need; I have kept it clean."

"Do you mind if we have a look? Besides, I need to get his clothes for him."

Irma shrugged her shoulders, "Go ahead."

They carted the cleaning implements up the stairs, 'just in-case'.

The room was merely functional; there was not even a picture to adorn a wall. A bureau with a mirror, a chair, and a small table filled the wall space around the twin-size bed.

The finger Josie ran over the dresser came up clean. Irma was on the job.

Violet smiled, anticipation in her eyes. Saturdays were reserved for jumping rope and kicking the can.

Josie opened the two small drawers at the top of the bureau. Underwear and socks were in one of the drawers; the other held writing paper, pencils, a ruler, and a notebook. Josie glanced through the notebook and then picked up a pencil and began writing on a piece of paper. Violet peered down on the notebook, "Mama, why are you copying those addresses?"

"Go, ask Irma for a bag to put Uncle Val's clothes in."

Josie was surprised at the number of alki-cookers that Val was in charge of. One of the participants was her own next-door neighbor.

Charlie P called an emergency meeting. The abandoned mill was selected as the venue. Six a.m. was set as the time, since there was less traffic, pedestrian as well as vehicle.

The participating members sat shivering in their coats, most of them unshaven, not a smile or a hint of civility among them. Sergeant McDermott got their attention.

"I have the list of names of the new unit of officers that will be patrolling Frankford and Bridesburg, not a Pollack among them. On the good side, two of them, Bob Aldrich and Steve Ginnis are formerly of the Passyunk unit, and appreciate the bonus perks they got used to under Johnny De. They're on board. Now, I'd like to offer them a little extra, for what I call the 'grousing agenda'. They'll zone in on any negative comments from the other cops and milk it until they see an opening for an introduction to a better way of life. These two cops are super intelligent, and I rely on them to bring the others around. I'll keep you informed of the progress."

Charley picked up on the positive attitude McDermott's message conveyed.

"The alki-cookers are surprisingly holding their own. Of course, that's due to the new unit being unfamiliar with the neighborhood and the residents. But our important clients with the moola are expecting their regular orders of Canadian. We can't use the Burlington Island pick up station because Butler has his small craft patrolling the Island."

He looked out at his audience. He was putting them to sleep, so he'd have to come up with a punch-line.

"There's a thirty-foot flat-top yacht I have my eye on, but we have to grab it fast! The owner has to leave the area in a hurry. We can buy it for twenty-two thousand dollars. That's a good ten thousand dollars less than market price. This is a vitally important matter that has to be acted on quickly."

Dobrowski called out, "What the hell are we gonna do with a yacht? Who the hell is the sailor in this bunch?"

Trawinski echoed the concern, "Are you crazy?"

"How 'bout you let me finish explaining my plan?" He arched his brows and tilted his head, an irksome twist of his lips, "With the profit we could make off of our Canadian liquor customers, we'll have the craft paid off in a month's time. Then, it's all profit."

"Where you gonna dock it? On the Delaware?" Dobrowski again, "And like I said; where you gonna get a sailor?"

"I got that all lined up. Harry Cusack's restaurant sits on the shoreline in Somers Point, Jersey, out of range of Butler's invading forces. There's a strong fishing pier on his property; we'll keep the boat docked there. Harry will use it as a speakeasy during the evening, behind the three-mile limit. We'll use it during the night to pick up booze from the Canadian Schooner," he chuckled, "what could be better?"

Murmurs of satisfied agreement rounded the room.

"What about the sailor?" Dobrowski asked.

"Harry's nephew was an Ensign in the Navy during the war. He knows his way around deep water and how to captain a yacht."

The furniture in the parlor was over thirteen years old. Not only was it out of style, but it was downright ratty-looking. Josie loved her home and had managed to purchase lace curtains and doilies to give the home a proper warmth. The kitchen posed no problem. The gas stove was in good condition and the icebox, well, what could you want from an icebox? It held ice and drained well. But the parlor! Josie thought a player piano would amuse her as well as Violet, and it was a piece of furniture that would add class to the room.

She had gained a certain reputation among the locals as 'the' interpreter that could win your case. She was in great demand, but this was not made evident in her paycheck. Her value was rewarded by the individuals who were fortunate enough to obtain her services; they were extravagant with their gratuities. The salary she earned from Pilsudski Union enabled her to maintain her table and pay the household bills, but the parlor's pallor could not be tolerated.

The list of Valentine's alki-cookers provided a benevolent resource. Gregor Potopski on Bermuda Street was her first benefactor. His satisfaction with the 'not guilty' verdict induced him to grant a twenty-five dollar tip to his skillful interpreter.

During her last appearance as interpreter in the Justice of the Peace court, Josie introduced herself to the attending police officer, Bob Aldrich, one of the new men on the beat. Once they understood each other's financial perspective, a casual partnership unfolded.

Josie was now *'on the take.'* She opened a savings account for her future parlor project.

CHAPTER 35

RELATIONSHIPS

Dawn approached the Polish neighborhoods, softly with an air of solemnity to grace a bounty of azaleas, roses, rhododendrons, and forget-me-nots. The first rays of light found many residents already up and about on this breezy Saturday in June 1925. A balmy seventy-six degrees began the day; humidity not yet in the offing.

Eddie Dobrowski stood under the oak tree in his backyard and allowed his emotions to play at the strings of his heart. He was in a tender, appreciative mood. At 2:00 p.m., the altar of St. John's church would play host to a variety of scents and colors in the pots and vases of flowers that adorned the altar. Garlands decorated the pews. The stage was reverently set for the exchange of vows that would bind Eddie and Teresa until death do them part.

After lunch, Father Churak took up his breviary to sanctify the morning in prayer. He was in the middle of Psalm 119 when a blast of music ripped through the floorboards. Jazz was infiltrating the entire first floor. Father laid his breviary on the lamp table and made his way to the basement. On the stairway down, the music grew louder, and laughter accompanied the cacophony.

"Aha! So, boys, how is the work coming?"

The youngsters practically stood at attention. A New York radio station was blaring jazz; one of the boys ran over to the table and turned off the radio. A few of the eighth-grade boys, who were also altar boys, had volunteered to arrange the tables for the afternoon nuptial celebration. Their effort would glean an invitation to the reception and the food and fun.

Father chuckled, "Okay, boys, it's Saturday and you're doing a great service, enjoy your music; I'll go to the garden to finish my prayers."

The arrangement of tables, including the buffet table was left to the church; catering was left to the café. Val was helping Maczek and Charlie's wife, Bianca with the final preparation of the menu that began atop the stove and roasted in the oven the day before; *gołąbki, bigos, kielbasa, pierogi, Bapkas*, ham, fresh baked rye bread, rolls, roasted chickens, salads, fruit, and of course *chruszicki.*

As this was to be a lively celebration, the wine would flow as the River Jordon within the dispensation allowed religious ceremonies. The source of abundance was duly provided for with the compliments of Charlie P and company.

Maczek was yielding to the tediousness of the preparations; he felt the need to change focus; he helped himself to a couple of shots of vodka from the bottle he and Valentine had been sharing.

"Valenti, who are you taking to the wedding?"

Val shot a querulous glance his way, "No one!"

Charlie picked up on the gibe, "What? Don Juan doesn't have a date?"

Val offered a solicitous smile, "I don't need a date, the women will be standing in line for a Polka with me."

Maczek scoffed, "Pardon me, Valentino!"

"Besides, I've been thinking, I just might become a priest and offer my manhood to God!"

The smell of incense mingled with the variety of flora distributed around the church became pervasive by two o'clock that sultry afternoon. The overhead fans whirled, and the women were brushing fans across their faces. Mendelssohn's March alerted the audience to the significance of the occasion. Eddie stood stiff as a Swiss Guard at the Vatican, seemingly unaware of the heat, more aware of the seriousness of the situation. Val stood next to him, joking in an effort to relax the groom before the bride made her march down the aisle. The procession began with four adorable five to eight-year-old girls dropping flowers as they walked. Teresa's sister, the maid of honor, wore a lovely gown of lavender, gowns of pale pink were worn by her bride's maids.

Behind this pastel display, the bride caught everyone's attention in her lavishly laced gown of white satin and a veil delicately crowned with silk violets. Eddie's first glance of the maidenly white appearance of his beloved melted away the tension, and he was filled with the tender warmth that he felt earlier that day in the garden.

The "Do you take this man?… I Do," and "Do you take this woman?… I Do," were announced and the priest entwined the wedding band around the couple's wrists. They were committed for life.

CHAPTER 36

RECEPTION

Steve Leonik's Top Hat Trio was warming up on stage while the wedding guests mingled about the room in search of empty tables. Delicacies awaited them on the banquet tables. Amid the potted flowers that were relocated from the chapel, a large bottle of wine sat aerating at every table.

Officer Ted Ginnis scanned the room to locate his patrol partner, Virgil Casey. The midnight shift required two patrolmen to ensure that at least one pair of eyes would be open during peak hours of illicit alcohol traffic. Ginnis had been skillfully conditioning Virgil, who had been transferred from the wealthy area of Philadelphia, Chestnut Hill. The residents there were aloof, and alcohol was not an issue; they could lay their hands on Canadian imports discreetly in Center City where most of them earned their hefty income. Ginnis saw the wedding reception as a graduation exercise. He had been employing McDermot's "grousing agenda." Ginnis played father confessor to Casey's gripes, discreetly offsetting them with positive tidbits of the benefits that were available in his new assignment. That was when a third officer, Bob Aldrich, dropped by the table to add reinforcement to the project.

Poles are excessively friendly at traditional celebrations; vodka brings out the benevolence of their nature. Virgil Casey was being bathed in brotherhood and beverage. He had never tasted Polish food before, and he was on an epicurean adventure.

After his toast of vodka, Aldrich caught sight of Josie dancing a Polka with her brother, Valentine; they were the best couple on the floor. His partners followed his gaze.

"That's Josephine Godowska, she interprets for the neighbors who are not proficient in English. A good woman." The Polka ended and Aldrich waved her over to the table."

"Well, don't you strike up an appearance!"

Her little black dress was sleeveless with a low-cut V neckline that tapered at the waist with a pleated skirt. It addressed every curve in her well-stacked body. Her shoes were black and white Spectators. The precision angle-cut bob was the perfect frame to enhance the high cheekbones on her oval face and firm chin.

"It's a celebration, I'm trying to outshine the bride." She took the seat of the chair that Aldrich proffered her. "Hello, Bob, business and pleasure?"

"No, purely pleasure. Butler would keel over at the sight of all this booze!"

"Josie, you know Officer Ginnis," Ginnis nodded his head and smiled, "and this is one of our new patrolmen, Virgil Casey, who is just getting acquainted with the denizens of Little Poland."

"Welcome, Officer, how are the folk treating you?"

"I never felt this welcome in my post in Chestnut Hill. The food is great, and I'm just learning of the benefits of vodka, Poland's national drink."

Officer Ginnis smiled appreciatively, and Officer Aldrich shot him a look that reflected, *job well done.*

Val was actively ingratiating himself while he mingled through the crowd. Leonik caught sight of him and snickered, "Valenti, come on up here and say hello to everyone with a song."

Leonik grinned and shook his head when Val named the tune, *"It Had To Be You,"* followed up with *"Everybody Loves My Baby."*

The bride and groom and a few couples left their platters and wine to dance to the tribute.

It was during his rendition of *"Everybody Loves My Baby"* that a temptingly plump derriere waltzed directly past him. He let his eye travel up to a head full of blonde wavy hair. He couldn't quite make out the face, but there was the whole day ahead of him.

Once the wedding cake was sliced and served, many of the guests left their family seating to socialize among their friends and acquaintances. Trawinski, Dobrowski, and Stabetski cozied up at the bar with Charlie P.

Trawinski poured from his bottle of vodka, "To open seas!"

"Na Zdrowia!" rounded out the toast.

"Na Zdrowia!" the other three men responded enthusiastically.

Stabetski opened the talk, "I hear Valentine has developed sea legs?"

Charlie ran his hand over his mouth after he downed his shot of vodka, "Yep, he sure has, he's a real Popeye the Sailor Man."

They all got a chuckle out of the comparison. Charlie went on, "It's the best thing we did, buying that boat. We're operating freely—Jersey's police force is rather lax in carrying out the Volstead Act. There's enough money going around to keep law enforcement happy."

"Aha!" Dobrowski noted a familiar figure coming their way. "Pour another shot, Trawinski, here comes McDermott."

"Michael, my man, how goes it with Butler at the wheel?" Charlie's way of greeting.

McDermott pursed his lips and shook his head, "That son-of-a-bitch is a diabolical insurgent!" He drained his glass, sucked in his lips, "He's making lots of enemies with the Republican politicians who like their glass of booze. Kendrick is still his cohort, but the police captains are straining under his invasion tactics. I don't know how this is going to end."

Val came down from the stage and scanned the room until he found the object of his eye. She was seated at a table of five indistinguishable people; only her blonde hair and round hazel eyes were prominent. There was a dimple in her cheek when she flashed a toothy smile. That smile implied a witty, playful character within. Val angled his way around tables and wandering guests.

"*Dzien dobry, Panienka,* when the band comes back from intermission, may I have the first dance?"

"How do you know what the first number will be? It could be a Mazurka, a Polka..." Her voice was a clear alto, with a mirthful intonation.

"It doesn't matter—Foxtrot, Waltz, Tango, I do them all well!"

Snickers went around the table; she beamed a delighted smile. "Would you mind introducing yourself, Mr. Dancer?"

"Ah, yes," he bowed low, "Valenti Pancross at your beck and call."

She offered her hand, and he kissed it, "Bianca Morowska, delighted to have you at my beck and call. "I hope the first number is a two-step, because that is my best dance."

The reception continued the following day, enough food and vodka remained, and the Top Hat Trio was available. Valentine got his two-step dance with Bianca, and Patrolman Casey added a new phrase to his vocabulary, *Na Zdrowia!*

CHAPTER 37

NOVEMBER

The weatherman predicted snow for Thanksgiving. There was an early chill in the air. Charlie's Café was celebrating the season with vigor. It had been a most fortunate year for the alcohol endeavor exploited by the neighborhood network. The Jersey enterprise was conducted with a steady stream of profit, and the alki-cookers were operating with little duress. Since there was no patron saint for wine, it must have been the Roman god Bacchus that shielded the covert operations.

Sergeant Michael McDermott doffed his cap and hung it on the coat rack. He was going to enjoy a leisurely breakfast. He had good reason to celebrate. He hefted his portly body onto the stool.

"Maczek, me boy, you've outdone yourself with the turkey decorations! Order me the triple threat breakfast, I'm tired of dieting."

The triple threat breakfast consisted of bacon and eggs, waffles with maple syrup, *pierogi and pączki* with coffee to wash it all down. It could adequately serve a family of four.

Charlie P came in through the back door and burst into laughter when he saw the spread on the counter and the customer who was about to indulge himself.

"What the hell is it, McDermott? You planning to leave the planet in a hurry?"

"Well, Smart Ass, you might very well want to celebrate the auspicious occasion that prompted me to give vent to such an indulgence. Butler is leaving us."

Maczek yelled, "Yippee!" Charlie stood still, trying to wrap his brain around the unexpected comment. McDermott went on..

"He sealed his exit warrant by closing down the lounges of the Bellevue Stratford and the Ritz-Carlton."

"Holy Shit!" Charlie audibly exhaled, "Maczek, vodka!"

The tug-of-war that had engaged Philadelphia during Butler's reign as Director of Public Safety came to an end on 22 December 1925. Police captains were squirreling away 'incentive' payments; magistrates were showing leniency for individuals caught in the act of illicit alcohol production; speakeasies were being warned prior to expected raids. It was business as usual, money was rolling in.

Brigadier General Smedley Butler, recipient of sixteen medals, five of which were presented for heroism; he is the only Marine to be awarded the Marine Corps Brevet Medal, as well as two Medals of Honor.

His farewell statement put his experience into perspective: "Cleaning up Philadelphia was worse than any battle I ever saw." He referred to Philadelphia as the "cesspool of Pennsylvania."

A plaque remains at the north portal of City Hall, from the north Broad Street entrance:

**"Brigadier General Smedley Butler,
Director of Public Safety, 1924-25."**

The economy appeared to be exploding, manufacturing had increased, consumers were relishing the new cars and the ready-made clothes lining the racks of the department stores. Lack of police action against illegal alcohol was adding tax-free money to the pockets of officers. One police captain had twenty-seven thousand dollars hidden under his bedroom rug. It was indeed the roaring twenties.

CHAPTER 38

AFTERMATH

August 1929 was as hot as hell. Frigidaire introduced air conditioning for home use, but only the wealthy could afford the bulky units. Overhead fans and closed windows during peak afternoon hours was the only available relief.

Felix Kaczynski was helping to unload his stock delivery when he doubled over in pain and fell to the ground, unconscious. An ambulance transported him to the hospital where he was diagnosed as having suffered a stroke. Fortunately, the hospital had an effective air conditioning system that kept the rooms cool. The oppressive heat could have wiped him out.

Kaczynski's grocery store was one of the busiest establishments in the neighborhood. Felix's wife, Maja, was left to handle the business on her own. She had help from her brother Adrian, but neither one of them could cut a rib steak from a loin of beef, nor was there anyone in the area who could fill-in. She phoned the meat packing company and cancelled their upcoming order, then she went to the walk-in freezer to assess what cuts of meat were left on the racks. It would be a bumpy road.

The air conditioning unit in Charlie's Café was paying for itself by increasing business. Maczek appreciated the increased amount of tips he raked in every day.

Customers looked upon eating at the café in the same light as going to see a movie - a place where you could be comfortable and forget about the heat. Even Eddie Dobrowski showed up once in a while. Teresa was the good Polish housewife, and an excellent cook. However, the Dobrowskis could not afford air conditioning, nor would his father consider installing it in the hardware store, saying, "We have enough fans!"

Eddie had spent the morning on alki-cooker rounds, his clothes were sweaty and clung to his body. He felt an unquenchable thirst—respite was needed immediately.

He opened the door to the café, the rush of cool air elicited an audible sigh, and *"Dzięki Bogum!"*

There was scattered tittering and sporadic comments:

"Look what the heat blew in!"

"Is Teresa on strike?"

He ignored the comments and walked directly to the counter, where Maczek had placed a glass of cold water and a menu before he took a seat on the stool.

"The special, Maczek, whatever it is."

Charlie was snickering on his way over to welcome him, "Don't let them rattle you, Edju."

Eddie guzzled his glass of water, laid the glass down on the counter, and wiped his mouth with the back of his hand; Emily Post be damned!

A small bucket sat on the counter with an attached band, "For Felix Kaczynski."

Eddie looked at the sign, then at Charlie, who nodded, "He had a stroke. Maja's beside herself, neither she nor Adrian knows a damned thing about butchering. We're trying to offer a cushion for her when she discovers all the bills coming due."

Maczek served the plate of ham sandwich and potato salad, the lunch special; Eddie nodded his appreciation, "Who's going to cut the meat for them?"

"That's the thing! Nobody seems to know a butcher."

Eddie pursed his lips and nodded, "I do!"

Charlie threw him a blank look.

"Teresa's Uncle Mike."

Charlie squinted, "Was he at the wedding?"

Eddie shook his head, "No, his wife had just passed away, leaving him with two children, a girl, I think about twelve, and a boy, seventeen. They live with their grandmother."

"How come I never heard about these guys?"

"They live in New York, Brooklyn."

"Listen, don't say anything about this, it may not be the answer to the problem, and we don't want to get Maja's hopes up. Check it out with Teresa and get back to me."

Valentine Pancross had moved into a newly structured apartment in Josephine's home. How much space did she and Violet need? The second floor already had a bathroom, so it was just a matter of installing kitchen appliances in one of the bedrooms and dragging the old furniture that was stored in the basement upstairs for a prospective tenant. Valentine applied and the deal was done; Josie had money she could count on to pay her bills, and Valentine had a home of his own.

Eddie dropped by with a top-of-the-shelf bottle of vodka as a housewarming gift.

"This is lovely," he commented, as he scanned the homey apartment, "but how are you going to manage your busy dating schedule under your sister's roof?"

"Edju, the women I date have establishments of their own."

"Come on, Val, you're not interested in a decent girl to fill your love life?"

"I don't trust decent women. I'm a happy, comfortable bachelor. And the added attraction of living here with Josie is that she's a good cook. What else could I ask for?"

"Na Zdrowia!" They downed their shot glasses, Eddie wiped his mouth with his hand, "We have a relative coming to stay with us, from New York."

"Teresa's uncle?"

"Yeah, he might be interested in the deal if Maja is desperate enough to offer him what he wants, which is a lot more than what he's earning in Brooklyn."

"How's it look right now?"

"Hmm, we may be stuck with him for a while. She's offered him almost double what he's earning now, and she added an extra incentive, two percent of the gross meat sales—the more he sells, the more he earns. He's a master butcher; he studied his trade in the old country, Poland and Germany."

"Wow! That's something. Listen, you don't have to be stuck with him; my old room at Walczak's is available."

Eddie shook his head, "No, Teresa loves him, and I enjoy his company. He's a friendly old codger. We'll see."

Michael Szymborski maintained a relaxed stance in his 5'8" frame. His slightly rounded shoulders did not detract; rather, they offered a degree of humbleness to the portly frame that suggested a fondness for food. His high cheekbones, firm chin, deep-set blue eyes, and curly light brown hair cast him in the image of a matinee idol.

His appearance had an immediate effect on Maja Kaczynski—it would have the same effect on her female customers.

Charlie P switched the card hanging on the front door from OPEN to CLOSED.

Maczek transformed the counter to its original function—a bar, where he stacked bottles of beer, wine, and vodka. Valentine and Eddie were in the kitchen preparing sandwiches for gnashing. There was a bittersweet atmosphere in the café. McDermott was retiring, a long-standing, solid relationship was coming to an end; the end of an era, actually.

Everything was ship-shape for the celebration. The members of the bootlegging network began to show up for booze and camaraderie; Trawinski was first, followed by Stabetski and Dobrowski. They grabbed a beer and waited for the guest of honor to appear for a toast with vodka.

When McDermott walked through the door, they sang the Polish birthday song, *Sto Lat.*

Sto lat, sto lat, niech zyia, zyia, nam! May you live a hundred years!

McDermott was a little unsteady in his gait, and a misty gleam came to his eyes,

"God Bless you Pollacks," and then he broke into song, "Oh, Danny Boy…"

And the Pollocks joined in the maudlin tune, not one of them macho enough to keep from sobbing.

Bob Aldrich took over the position of sergeant. Michael McDermott planned to invest his "bonus" profit in the purchase of a family home at the Jersey Shore.

September remained hot and humid. Now and then, a rainy day would break the pattern, and a northerly wind would call for a sweater to be worn. But by the middle of the month, crisp mornings and falling leaves brought a sense of vim and vigor to the scene.

Val's appetite was sharpening, and he requested *gołąbki* for Sunday dinner. Violet added an enthusiastic, "Yes!" Josie nodded in agreement.

As soon as Saturday morning chores were completed, Josie and Violet trundled off to Kaczynski's with their grocery baskets nestled in the crook of their arms.

One look at the line in front of the butcher block and Josie regretted her penchant for neatness; she should have let the chores go.

Adrian noticed her tapping her foot and sucking in her lips, signs of a possible eruption. He made his way through the crowd to circumvent her typical loud verbal reaction.

"Josie, why don't I pick up the items on your list while you wait your turn in line?" She gave him a blank stare, then handed him her list and basket.

The new butcher was carving his way around a loin cut of pork, "So, what do you think, Battalino or Routis?" He had an odd accent, Polish sprinkled with Brooklynese.

The man who was admiring the finesse of the carver picked up on the topic with apparent interest, "Battalino, look what he did to the Cuban!"

"Tak, tak, the Americans are better boxers, look at Tunney, he KO'd Jack Dempsey twice!"

"What's going on here? A butcher shop or a bookie's parlor?" Josie was at it.

The man moved aside, the butcher smiled sweetly, "What's the matter, *Piękna Pani, (Beautiful lady)* you don't like prize fighting?" He gave her his full attention.

There were mixed comments from the customers standing by. One gentleman remarked, "You're right, Mike, Battalino's gonna take the featherweight title."

Adrian had filled her basket and laid it on the bench, just as she moved up to the butcher block.

"How can I help you, *Piękna Pani?*"

"Never mind the *Piękna Pani,* give me two pounds of ground pork."

"For *gołąbki?*"

"What do you care what for?"

"Because, *Pani,* if I mix in beef and veal, you'll get a better pot of *gołąbki.*"

She twisted her lips and gave it a thought. "Alright," she condescended.

She ordered cold-cuts for sandwiches, and while he was slicing the ham, he paused the slicer, took a slice and handed it to Violet, *"Piękna Panienka,* here, try this."

Violet looked to Josie and then reached out for the sample, *"Dziękuję Pan."*

"You're a lovely lady, like your Mama," he said as he handed Josie a slice of the ham.

She sucked in her lips to prevent a smile, took the ham, and then let the smile loose, "Thank you."

As they were leaving the store, Mike called out, *"Piękna Pani,* do you invite me to taste your *gołąbki* this Sunday?"

This time she burst out laughing.

CHAPTER 39

POKER

Saturday night, Val was amusing Violet with their weekly game of gin rummy. Josie was in the kitchen, clearing away the after-dinner remnants of cold cuts and potato salad.

Val had his bottle of home-brew, and Violet was sipping her root beer. They were vying over cards in the game of Gin. Val had wiped away three games, he looked at his watch—time to let Vi get a winning hand, tonight was poker night. Vi laid down a card, picked up another from the discard pile, and knocked. Val threw up his hands, "You sure you didn't cheat?" Vi tittered.

He finished his brew, replaced the cap on the empty bottle, "Say, Josie?"

"Co?" ("What?") she asked, her lips rounded out the soft 'ts' sound of the Polish 'c'. She knew the tone of an oncoming request.

"Is it all right if I bring a poker buddy of mine to dinner tomorrow? He loves Polish food; he's a boarder at Walczak's."

"It's your home, why ask?"

Sunday morning, after mass, followed the usual routine. Val prepared the toast and coffee, Vi set the table, and Josie prepared *kielbasa* and eggs. A head of cabbage was left cooking on the stove while they ate. Everyone had a cleanup duty before Val and Vi could sit down to the Sunday funnies. Both the *Record* and the *Inquirer* were scattered around the living room. Val's greatest pleasure was the 'funnies'. When he was forced to go to Poland as a boy, he begged Josie to send him the weekly comic strips.

Josie busied herself with the preparation of *gołąbki*. At noon, she plucked a rolled cabbage out of the steaming pot of sauce; she sliced off a piece with her fork for a taste. Her eyebrows lifted, she smacked her lips, "That butcher was right, this is delicious!"

Precisely at one o'clock, the front door opened, and two male voices carried the traditional greeting, *"Niech będzie pochwalony Jesús Chrystus!"*

Josie called from the kitchen, *"Na wieki wieków, Amen."* She wiped her hands in her apron as she approached Val and his guest who carried a dozen red roses and a sheepish grin.

"Oh, my God, it's the butcher!"

Mike chose his seat next to Violet. He focused a paternal interest on her by filling her plate before his own. "How old are you, Violet?" his tone thickly accented in his mixture of Polish and Brooklynese.

"Eighteen," she proudly announced.

"Eighteen! You're a young lady, and a beautiful one too."

Josie was observing all of this with a critical eye—Val was involved in sauce and *gołąbki*.

"I have a little girl, Irena is her name, she is twelve."

"Where is she?"

"In New York, with her *Babcia*. I miss her so. I also have a beautiful boy, Stanley. He is seventeen, also living with *Babcia*."

Val paused long enough between helpings to change the subject. "How are things going for you at Kajzinski's"

"Good, I have no complaints."

"What about your customers?"

"The same. I find people are the same everywhere, they want the best they can get for their money. Me too, I want the best."

He turned his attention to Josie, "*Pani*, you are an excellent cook, and I can see by your home, that you are a good homemaker. It must be difficult for you to keep all this going without a husband. Do you work too?"

Val answered for her, "She's a lawyer, she goes to bat for Poles who have a problem with the English language and understanding the law."

Josephine's belly shook with laughter, "I'm an interpreter for people who find themselves in trouble, people who are members of the Pulaski Union where I work."

It was an evening to relax. Val had spent the day at sea loading cases of Canadian Wine and Bermuda Rum. Josie had two court cases to interpret/arbitrate, and Vi had finished her algebra homework. Amos and Andy's antics entertained them in the background while Val sipped a brew and Josie pulled on her needle and thread as she embroidered the border of a bedroom doily.

During a commercial break, Val cleared his throat, "Josie, I bet Mike really misses his little girl."

Josie stopped stitching and looked over at Vi, *"Hmm*—I'm sure he does."

"He only gets to see her on Sundays."

Josie nodded her head.

"How bout we invite them for dinner this Sunday?"

Josie leaned back in her chair, took another look at Vi, and nodded her consent.

Val was on his usual delivery of cooked alcohol and Canadian Wine for Johnny De's speakeasy. It was Johnny's fourth operation in one year; Butler had closed the other three.

The club was dark. The only light came from Johnny's favorite table where he was clicking and clacking away on his adding machine. Duke Ellington's *"Cotton Club Stomp"* was on the turntable.

"Hey, what are you, a CPA or a bar owner?"

"Val, baby, pour yourself an espresso at the bar and come on over here."

A steaming cup in hand, Val took the seat opposite Johnny.

"You got stock, Val?"

Val wrinkled his nose, "Stock! Are you kidding? I got a small savings account."

"You could still buy stock. You could buy it on margin."

Val pushed his cap back. "What the hell's that?"

"It's a great way to get started. You take your savings and place them in a margin account; I got a broker who will do it for you. You can borrow on the account. When your stock rises, you can pay back the loan or use the profit to buy more. The only way you can get hurt is if your stock falls, then you gotta pay the piper."

"So, you play the stock market?"

"Yeah Man, how else you think I kept going after my run-ins with Butler. The market's going wild. You can't believe how much money I've made. Better than playing the horses."

He picked up the *Inquirer*, "Look." The headlines read, "Stocks Take To Sea."

"The New York Stock Exchange gave a couple of brokers permission to take quotes aboard ships, by radio. This is going worldwide!"

Val gave the matter considerable thought on his ride back home.

He arrived at Charlie's office to turn in the cash he got from Johnny De. His mind was still preoccupied with the prospects of getting rich on the stock market.

"Charlie, you got stock?"

"I got what?"

"Stock, you know, the stock market."

"Listen, Valenti, I don't trust the banks. They lend your money to other people. I don't know anything about the stock market, or do I care to."

"Johnny says I could open a margin account with my savings and buy stocks with loaned money."

"That's already too complicated for me. I work damn hard for my money, and I want to keep it nearby where I can protect it. Where you got your savings?"

"In my sock drawer."

"That's close enough. Keep it there."

CHAPTER 40

COMPASSION

It was just after breakfast on Sunday morning. The table was cleared, and the funnies were spread on the living room floor. Josie was working on a pot of *bigos,* a stew of pork, sauerkraut, and potatoes. The doorbell rang and Josie cocked an ear to hear the expected guests.

Mike was as giddy as a teenage girl as he introduced his daughter to Val and Violet. Josie took a quick look in the mirror, arranged her hair, and untied her apron.

"Good morning, Irena, have you had breakfast?"

"Yes, *Pani, Tatush* took me to the Automat."

"Wow! That's a treat!" Violet was impressed, "Have you read the funnies yet?"

The tiny, thin blonde shook her head, "No."

"Here, I'll get you Orphan Annie!"

Val sat in his chair, smiling at them. Mutt and Jeff lay open on his lap.

Josie looked over at Mike, who stuck out like a sore thumb, grinning.

"Mike, you want a cup of coffee?"

He looked at Josie, still grinning, *"Tak, tak, bardzo dziękuję!"*

He followed her into the kitchen, "Ahh, you make *bigos!"*

Josie pulled a cup and saucer from the china closet and poured the coffee.

"Your little girl is beautiful. She seems shy."

"Tak, she still grieves for her Mama."

"What about your son?"

"Ahh, Stashu is going to join the army, he wants security. He's a smart boy; he might be able to make something of himself."

Val joined them in the kitchen. Vi took Irena upstairs to her bedroom.

Irena's eyes grew large as she took in the maple furnishings of the pink and purple bedroom, "You have your own radio?"

Violet was surprised by the remark; she merely nodded a 'yes'.

Irena sat in the big oak rocking chair and Violet hopped on the bed.

"What's it like in New York?"

Irena shrugged her shoulders, "Okay."

"Do you like your school?"

"Not much, I have no friends. Sometimes I hide in the closet instead of going to school."

"What does your *Babcia* say about that?"

"The truant officer came to the house, and she beat me in front of him."

"Oh, my God!"

"I hate my *Babcia.*"

Chicory coffee and *pączki* held center stage at the breakfast table, where a getting-to-know-you session was being held.

"Mike, you're fortunate to have your mother-in-law willing to care for your kids." Josie offered, in a sympathetic tone.

He tipped his head to the right and nodded, *"Tak,"* followed by a deep sigh, "she's not an easy woman. My wife, Doretka, told me many stories of how she treated her when she was a kid. He ran his finger over the rim of the cup, "Irena also complains. Stashu wants me to sign for him to go in the service; he can't wait to be eighteen." He raised his right hand in a *'so...'* gesture.

Val and Josie looked down at their cups as the bigos slowly steamed on the stove.

Mike and Irena left directly after dinner. It was a two-hour ride to New York, and Mike had to ride back to Philly to be at work in the morning.

Violet had homework to finish while Val and Josie relaxed in the living room. They were unable to shake the gloom left by Mike's tale of woe.

"That's a hell of a thing for that little girl." Val's eyes reflected an emotion he was feeling, "We know what that's like, Josie."

Their mother, Olga, was a brutal parent. None of her children ever felt kindness or love. What they did feel was the strap and the shouting.

Josie seemed apprehensive. Finally, "Violet, come down here a minute."

Violet entered, ready for a command.

"Violet, would you consider having Irenka as a roommate?"

"Oh, yes, Mama, she hates her *Babcia*; I feel so sorry for her."

A single-size bed was ordered from the Capital Furniture Store on Front Street. Josie had enough bedding to cover the bed. A warm cotton quilt in pink and purple that matched the décor of Violet's bedroom was added to offer a touch of comfort. The leaves of the maple tree that sat outside the bedroom window were beginning to change colors. Irena would arrive in time to celebrate Halloween.

It was a pork roast with sweet potatoes that filled the plates for Sunday dinner. Irena's bags sat on the floor of the foyer—dinner first.

Mike was obsequious in his display of gratitude; Irena poked her fork through her food in a wary manner, causing Violet to appear apprehensive. She wondered, *Would Irena's presence bring gloom to the house?*

Monday morning, Mike walked Irena to St. John's. He had taken the morning off, telling Maja, "Take any meat orders and I will fill them as soon as I get back."

He had a pork roast tucked under his arm - it never hurt to juice up a new relationship.

They arrived as the children stood lined up for entrance, a nun kept order by walking in between the lines; several of the younger children were bold enough to call out to the new arrival, "What's your name?" "What grade are you in?" The nun blew her whistle, and everyone straightened up in line.

CHAPTER 41
TRANSITIONS

Irena slipped her hand under the doormat to retrieve the latchkey she was told to use in the event that no one was home when she returned from school. She opened the door and replaced the key. She went directly to the stairs and ran up to the bedroom, where she threw herself on the bed and cried herself to sleep.

Violet arrived home minutes before Josie was due from work. She ran into the kitchen and set the table before she went upstairs to change.

"Why are you so late?" Irena stopped rocking in the chair, an anxious look on her face.

Violet seemed stunned by the accusatory tone in her voice, "Why?"

Irena's face wrinkled into sobs.

"What's the matter, Irena?"

"Violet, the nun was terrible! She read the report from my school and said truancy was not acceptable in her school. *Tatush* had to beg her to take me in."

Violet put her arm around her, "Shush, don't cry. That nun had no right to talk that way in front of you. I know Sister Agnes, she's a mean woman!"

"I'm on probation; the first time I miss school, I'm out."

"Don't you worry, Irena. We'll get my Mom to go talk to her; she'll set her straight." She wrinkled her nose and narrowed her eyes, Irena burst into laughter.

"Violet, why were you so late?"

She sucked in her lips, a confidential smirk followed, "I was at Kumor's Sweet Shop with George. He got off early from work so we could meet."

"Who's George?"

"The man I'm going to marry. But that's a secret you must not share with anyone."

On Tuesday, Josie made a rare appearance at a weekday mass. Afterwards, she walked over to the school to have a chat with Sister Agnès. It was understood that Irena was now in her care, and there would be no unnecessary absences by Irena. If she were to miss time in class, there would be a valid reason, and Josie would sign a note of explanation.

After dinner that night, Josie assuaged Mike's concern for Irena's encounter with the nun.

"She'll be fine. She's going through a transition, and that's difficult, but she's young and strong. She'll get through it."

Valentine found himself free on Saturday night. There was a film at the Ritz that he was dying to see, *The Cocoanuts* with the Marx Brothers. After dinner, he offered to escort the girls to an evening of hilarity, at his expense.

Mike and Josie were left to share the Sunday *Inquirer,* which came on the stands after 6:00 pm Saturday. They took turns feeding the gramophone with their individual favorite discs. A bottle of vodka topped off the evening. Two happy people relaxing after a week's grueling work.

Mike finished his shot of vodka and got up to fetch the bottle for a refill. Ever the gentleman, he filled Josie's glass first. He handed her the glass and was taken aback by a soft, tender look on her face. He paused and then got down on his knees and began to kiss her hands, murmuring gentle phrases in Polish.

The evening was young, and there was no one at home.

CHAPTER 42
TUESDAY

The café was not yet open for business when the newsboy made his usual drop-off at Charlie P's. Charlie tucked it under his arm and walked to his usual seat at the counter. Maczek set the dish of *kielbasa* and eggs on the counter and went to pour a freshly brewed cup of coffee.

"Holy shit!" he reacted to the headlines,

**"Stocks Collapse in 16,410,030 Share Day,
But Rally at Close Cheers Brokers."**

He let his breakfast sit while he phoned Trawinski. "Get the phones going, we meet at Stabetski's in one hour, mandatory!"

Charlie watched them stumble in, groaning, Stabetski hadn't shaved.

"You read the headlines? This is sure to impact our business; there's sure to be a drop in sales. Anybody here got stock?"

"I do," a hoarse whisper from Trawinski.

"I do," Stabetski added.

"Well?"

"I don't know," there was anguish in Stabetski's tone, "I can't get a hold of my broker!"

Trawinski fretted, "I have the same broker."

The news media went on for the next week, offering headlines that conflicted with the reality of the dire situation:

"Wave of Buying Sweeps Over Market As Stocks Rally"
"Prominent Banker Says Boom Will Run Into 1930s"

Trawinski and Stabetski no longer had a portfolio.

For ten years, Josie had been in survival mode. Her marriage to Walek Godowski had not been a happy one. Walek's illness and the drinking problem that was brought on by the fumes that ate at his lungs in the ammonia factory caused anxiety and financial problems.

Left on her own, she had become a successful interpreter for the immigrants at the Pilsudski Union. She owned and maintained a well-organized home. Violet was doing well in high school, and Josie had developed the skills of a handyman. She even managed to repair her leaking roof. Josephine Godowski did not need a man.

Mike's gratitude knew no bounds. Saturdays had become provisions day. The ice box was filled with meat for the week, the larder's shelves were stocked with condiments and staples. He had become a regular at the table.

Val rarely made it home for dinner, and Mike's presence provided the table with a sense of security; his interest in the girls' daily activities provided fatherly comfort to them.

Josie was not only comforted but relieved from her normal focus of responsibility. Her emotions were heightened. She was gentler, her innate feminine instincts were on display. The girls tittered about her relaxed manner and her obvious deference to Mike's stabilizing effect.

Saturday nights were made to shake the grit of work off your shoes and enjoy the creature comforts the work week restricted. Mike and Josie enjoyed their favorite records, a bottle of vodka and each other's company far into the night.

Val carefully removed his shoes, and as stealthily as possible under the influence of a night's debauchery, climbed the stairs. It was almost dawn, and soon the girls would wake to the alarm clock to prepare for Mass. He was halfway up the stairs when he caught Mike leaving the bathroom.

The aroma of *kielbasa* and eggs hovered over the breakfast table where Josie, Mike, and Val were sipping coffee and sharing gossip.

Val got that shit-eating grin on his face, the devilish look in his eyes, "Say, Mike, didn't I see you come out of the bathroom this morning, before the kids woke up?"

Josie choked on the sip of coffee. Mike reddened and turned to look at Josie for defense.

Val chuckled, "Look, the girls know what's going on. You two aren't as cautious as you might think. Mike, why don't you just move in? I know the girls would appreciate having a father to protect them from Josie."

Tuesday evening, Irena led the blessing at the dinner table. During the passing of dishes, Josephine spoke out in her commander's tone, "I stopped at Kumor's for lunch today. It seems that you are a regular customer there, Violet!"

Irena held her fork midair. Mike looked on with mild interest. Violet blushed and froze.

"Well?"

There was no response.

"Who is this George?"

Violet looked down at her napkin, "A friend."

"What kind of friend?"

No response.

"How old is this friend?"

No response.

Mike interrupted the interrogation, "Valchia, give me your dish, I know you like mashed potatoes."

Violet's lips pulled to a slight appreciative smile as she handed him the plate.

"Josie, don't you think we should meet this fellow, George? Maybe ask him to dinner on Sunday?"

No response.

CHAPTER 43

DINNER

The kitchen withstood an invasion after Mass on Sunday. Mike was seasoning the eye round of beef, Josie was peeling potatoes and carrots, Valentine was tossing the ingredients for a salad, and the girls were cleaning up the dining room after breakfast. The open bottle of vodka made the whole operation seem less of a chore.

Valentine was singing along with the Polish radio station and, every now and then, someone else would join in on a verse.

George was coming to dinner.

The girls had the dining room table set with the best linen and tableware and were sitting in the living room, waiting for the doorbell to chime. The clock on the mantle chimed three bells and the doorbell gave its familiar tune. George had arrived.

Violet was rushing to the door when Valentine entered the hall, "Sit still, *dziecka,* let a man usher in the guest."

"*Niech bedzie pochwalonie Jesús Chrystus!*"

"*Na zawse, amen.*"

"Okay! A fellow Pole!"

The young man tittered.

"Welcome, I'm Valentine. You must be George!"

"Hello, Valentine," an amused smile presented a firm set of white teeth, a sharp jawline, and a wide chin that was topped by a thick head of brown hair. He wasn't very tall, but he was brawny, and he carried himself well.

"Call me Val. Come on in, they're all dying to meet you," he noticed the package in his arm. "What's that; you baked a pie?"

Violet was giggling and anxious, she walked over to George, "Here, George, let me take your coat."

"And I'll take your pie to the kitchen." Val relieved him of the package.

"Vi, take your friend into the kitchen and introduce him to your Mom."

Irena waved and smiled when they walked by. She had, by then, already met him at Kumor's.

Josephine gave an appreciative glance when they entered the room.

"George Kryzostoff, meet my mother, Josephine Godowski and our family's good friend, Mike Szymborski."

Josie seemed startled, "That's not Polish, that's Russian."

"Yes,' George smiled broadly.

Josephine sat down on the chair. She looked at the floor for a moment, she appeared bemused, then, "My maiden name was Kryszostanski."

"Your maiden name was Pancross!" Violet corrected her.

"No. That's what it became when your Grandfather came to America. He went to get a deed for the farm at the magistrate's office and the clerk figured out the meaning of the word *krysz*, cross, and he already had the word *Pan,* for Mr. written on the line, so he just added the Cross—Pancross."

Valentine guffawed. He had never heard the story.

Mike walked over to shake his hand, "Nice to meet you, young man."

During dinner, Val questioned the slight accent he heard in George's speech.

"My parents owned a restaurant in St. Petersburg. When the Archduke Ferdinand was assassinated in 1914, my father had the foresight to expect a war in Europe, so they sailed to Cherbourg and took an ocean liner to New York. Two years later, they became citizens. I was six years old when we left Russia. I thought I lost my accent. You have a good ear, Val."

"I'm a singer," he chortled.

The girls cleared the table, Josie set the percolator on for coffee and brought out the dessert plates and cups; an apple pie was taking center stage on the table.

"Horn and Hardart's apple pie," Mike made note, "from Kensington and Allegheny?"

George nodded, "I work there, I'm a short-order cook."

CHAPTER 44

1930

Johnny De found himself wading in deep waters. He lost his investments in the stock market that he had such faith in. The neighborhood of Passyunk, where he operated his speakeasy, was predominately a working class population which slowly began to react to growing unemployment ranks. Charlie P had extended him credit, but Johnny was dealing with a stark reality… he knew he was fighting a losing battle.

Charlie P was becoming more short-tempered; Maczek and Valentine were walking on eggs around him. Charlie was dipping into the Network's capital to extend credit to his most important customers. His cohorts were becoming increasingly agitated over his leniency and the possibility of financial ruin. Trawinski and Stabetski could count the gray hairs they had gleaned after their market losses.

By spring, Mike had become an integral part of the household; he had moved in bag and baggage. Val couldn't care less, Irena was happy to have her father sharing her new home, but a bit disturbed over the fact that he was sharing Josie's bed. Violet was livid.

Violet's graduation day offset any hostile feelings she had towards her mother and this man. She was overjoyed with the upcoming events of the day. George's parents had invited the entire family to their Russian Tea Room on Cottman Avenue, just two blocks away from Northeast High School.

George presented her with a corsage. Josie gave her a card with a hundred-dollar bill enclosed, Mike had a gold bracelet engraved with the date, and her Uncle Val purchased a large purse "for her to keep her wealth in." Irena drew a picture of her in a graduation cap and gown. She had graduated with honors.

Afterwards, her entire entourage walked the two blocks to the Russian Tea Room.

Fortunately, a table was reserved in her honor, as the place was crowded. The first impression of George's parents was sketchy at best. There were two waitresses serving the customers. Mr. and Mrs. Kryzostoff were in the kitchen preparing dishes that were a foreign delight to the neighborhood:

Pelmeni-the Russian version of *pierogi…,*

Blini-a Russian crepe…

Beef Stroganoff…

Kasha - an Eastern European staple, a pudding of mixed grains…

…and, of course, Russian Tea, served from two huge *samovars* that were placed on opposite sides of the red and green decorated room.

A huge plate of assorted cheeses held center place on the rectangular table set for six. George explained the significance of the cheese dish, "In Russia, cheese is a symbol of self-reliance, independent thinking, to offset the degrading image the peasant held under the rule of the Romanoffs. Milk and cheese were plentiful on the farms, and the farmers produced them for the wealthy. Ah, here come *Matka* and *Tata.*"

A couple attired in short sleeves and aprons approached the table. She, petite and slender with dark hair, raised in a bun at the back of her head, with dark brown, almond-shaped eyes and a maternal smile. He, an older version of George, also smiling.

George stood up to make the introductions. "Alina, my mother, and Dimitri, my father." Mike and Val respectfully stood up. "Violet, the graduate, her mother, Josephine, Valentine, her uncle, and Mike."

Dimitri extended his hand to the men, "*Privetek,*" he shook hands and then turned his attention to the ladies. "*Kak dela,*" he kissed Josie's hand, held Violet's hand, and rubbed Irena's head.

Alina tempeled her hands and made a brief bow, "Hello, everyone, so happy to meet Violet and her parents."

"Yes," said Dimitri, "but we must arrange a meeting where we can become more familiar with each other."

Josie extended the invitation, "When is your day off?"

In a duet, they replied, "Mondays."

"How about you, George?"

"I can make arrangements for next Monday."

CHAPTER 45

COMMITMENT

The 'getting to know you' dinner did not go well. Mike's place in the home proved disturbing to the Kryzostoffs, who were fervent in their faith of the Eastern Orthodox. It was an embarrassment for Josie, and Violet was incensed.

Josie spent a restless night dwelling on the disapproval she perceived from George's parents. She woke with a resolution— there would be a forthcoming commitment, or else!

Kaczynski's was operating at a decreased rate of profit. Meat sales were down. Customers were returning to the old country recipes that the peasants had lived on for centuries; meat was unaffordable. That the store remained afloat at all was due to the continued alki-cookers and necessary ingredients. It seemed the customers were less comfortable living without their alcohol.

So, when Mike requested a day off for some important business he had to attend to, it was easily granted.

Josie merely mentioned that she would need a day off, and *Pani* Nazdek nodded her head to acquiesce.

They were off to City Hall to acquire a marriage license.

Charlie P's leniency had to be dealt with. Trawinski and Stabetski called a meeting, and Charlie was included.

It was Stabetski's turf, so Stabetski took the lectern.

"Although it is a good thing to be tolerant and generous toward others, there is the matter of self-interest."

"Yeahs" came from the audience.

"Sales are ten to fifteen percent lower, and the way the market is going…it's going to get worse." He paused to get a sense of the reaction from the members.

"Let's take a vote on extending credit to our clients."

"All in favor of continuing credit, raise your hands."

Charlie gritted his teeth and tightened his lips, "Okay! I get the picture!"

He glanced at everyone in the room, "Stabetski, do we have to vote on getting a bottle of vodka out here?"

The air was cleared, and good fellowship resumed as the bottle made its rounds. In the middle of the drinking and joking, Eddie burst through the door,

"Val, Johnny De shot himself!"

CHAPTER 46

CAN YOU SPARE A DIME

Although the monthly membership dues at the Pilsudski Union cost no more than the price of a loaf of bread, most members preferred to spend the amount on bread. 1931 was proving more disastrous; how long could this go on?

Josie was on a commission basis, only cases involving alcohol were being tried, and with the minimal police activity, very few cases were brought before the magistrate.

Maja Kaczynski and Adrian sat at the table, the yearly receipts spread before them, Adrian deftly punching the keys on the adding machine. Mike had to go.

Val's contribution to the table and his monthly rent was all Josie could rely on; Violet had taken a job with Horn & Hardart, at the salad bar, and moved out.

Bigos with a small ham hock, potatoes, and black bread was the Thanksgiving Day feast that served the family of three at Josie's table. Val had been invited out.

Conversation was limited to, "Pass the…"

Mike was the only one to eat with an appetite; he always had an appetite. Josie had forgotten what it was like to be poor, and she didn't appreciate the occasion to provide her with a reminder. Irena missed the company of Violet at the table and doodled her way around her food. She asked to be excused and left her plate with hardly a dent in its contents. Mike and Josie finished their meal and cleared the kitchen with nary a word between them.

Alina and Dimitri Kryzostoff prepared a capon with sweet potatoes, green beans, and poppy seed rolls. A fresh green salad was tossed with a cheese dressing, the samovar was kept hot for the dessert of *ptiche moloko*, layers of silky custard spread between layers of sponge cake.

There were no customers to interrupt the fine dining.

Alina and Dimitri were unusually gregarious and relaxed. They told humorous and maudlin tales of cherished memories of Russia, a land they still loved and missed. Then Dimitri made an announcement.

"We are closing the Tea Room. We cannot afford the prices for food, and we have no customers."

Alina's eyes filled with tears, and George sprang from his seat to run to her side.

"Don't cry, *Matka*, everyone is in the dumps, there's no work and no money. We'll get through this, Violet and I are working, we'll make it, you'll see."

She wiped her eyes with her napkin and kissed his cheek.

Back on his seat at the table, he took Violet's hand,.

"I, too, have an announcement to make," George lowered his chin, raised his eyes in a sheepish grin, "You can rent Violet's room to Uncle Boris."

Confused looks were a response to the comment.

"Violet and I eloped last week."

Dimitri banged his fist on the table as Alina gasped. Dimitri went on to rave in Russian, the gist of it being, "What the hell is wrong with you? Were your mother and I not to preside at your wedding? Our only son?"

Violet was crying, George pulled her close to him and offered his defense, "This is no time for grand weddings, and I know that you and *Matka* would spend your last penny, and maybe even mortgage this building to pay for one."

He waited for them to absorb the reality of his remark

"When, and if, this depression ever ends, we'll go to the priest and have our marriage blessed. Then you can go on a spree."

There would be no tree in Josie's house this year. Val had offered to buy one and decorate it, but Josie was fixated on her current emotional doldrums.

Mike set up the manger on the living room tea table and hung a wreath on the door. He was ever more engaged in domestic tidiness due to his lack of employment. He maintained a spotless kitchen and even went so far as polishing everyone's shoes.

Josie was becoming increasingly vexed with his scouring the kitchen, scrubbing the floors, and his insistence on helping to prepare the meals. What was that old adage of two women in the kitchen?

Christmas Day found the two of them alone. Val was grateful for the invitation that Eddie and Teresa extended to him, and Irena begged Violet to let her celebrate Christmas at the Kryzostoffs.

There was a good reason for celebration at the now-defunct Tea Room. Dimitri had applied for a position at Horn & Hardart's. With his excellent resume and years of experience as a restaurateur, he was snatched up for the position of manager at the Eighth and Market Street site. Alina had applied for a spot in the bakery.

To celebrate the family's good fortune, everyone employed at a time of widespread unemployment, the typical Russian Christmas feast adorned the table.

Borscht made the first round, followed by *Sochivo*, a sweet porridge of grains, honey, poppy seeds, and nuts, symbolizing hope and prosperity. A stuffed goose, garnished with caviar, and the ever-present *Pirozhi/Pierogi.*

Violet made every effort to enjoy the meal, but the huge goose looming in front of her caused her to rush from the table. She made it to the bathroom in time to wretch in the toilet bowl.

Irena was the only one at table to seem confused by the action; wry smirks appeared on the faces of the others, with a look of concern in their eyes. Violet was pregnant.

CHAPTER 47

CONCESSIONS

There was frost in the air on Easter Sunday at the end of March in 1932. At the Fifth Avenue Parade, only the bedecked hats of the ladies displayed a flair for spring. Due to the alignment of the Julian calendar and the Gregorian calendar that year, *Paskha*, Russian Easter, would be celebrated on the same Sunday as its Catholic observance.

Violet's pregnancy was quite obvious. It didn't look as though many days would elapse before another Kryzostoff would join the family. Her discomfort displayed itself in her facial gestures and her ungraceful mobility.

The rare occasion of the mutual date of the Resurrection prompted Dimitri to invite Josie and Mike to the Tea Room. Everything in the restaurant remained intact in the cherished hope that one day the economy would once more make the enterprise a successful venture.

Now that the couple had married, they were no longer an affront to their religious convictions; Dimitri and Alina could afford to be magnanimous.

Saturday evening in the kitchen was actually a pleasant scene. Val chose to spend the evening at home, instead of his usual habitat of the speakeasy. Irena was looking forward to dinner at the Tea

Room, and Mike and Josie put aside their differences to engage in the traditional egg dying.

Saturday afternoon was spent at the stove and oven. Mike and Josie made a variety of *pierogi* to offer a taste contrast to the *pirozhi* that Dimitri and Alina would serve. Irena made a triple batch of *chrusciki*, Polish bow-tied cookies. Val's contribution was a canned Polish ham and three bottles of Canadian wine to commemorate the Lord's Last Supper event, the presentation of bread and wine. He knew there would be bread and *bapka* at the table.

Three tables were fitted together to accommodate the large party, each one decorated with an elaborately embroidered tablecloth that Alina had designed. There was a *Bapka,* or *Kulich,* served with a sweet cottage cheese. *Kulebiaka,* a layered fish pie with mushrooms and rice was the main course. After all, the Lord did spend his time with fishermen.

And, of course, colored eggs.

Josie's eyes lighted on Violet's figure and she shook off a feeling of trepidation. She had been a bit irregular and panicked at the thought of an unwanted and untimely pregnancy of her own. She would make an appointment with Dr. Wysczinski first thing in the morning.

Josie was on the third decade of her second rosary when the nurse announced her name; she had been praying for negative results.

Dr. Wysczinski was his usual early morning pleasant self. He completed his customary routine checkup of heart, lungs, throat, and ears and pulled his chair next to Josie, "So, what's your complaint?"

"I think I might be pregnant."

A bright smile spread on his face, he lowered his chin, looked up over his spectacles, "Josie, you're forty years old. You're probably going through the change. Let's not be ridiculous, let's just wait and see."

Poverty was not Josie's style, and an unemployed Mike under her feet was no longer tolerable.

Fortunately, Josie's mode of operation, anonymously phoning the police to raid an unsuspecting alki-cooker so that she could intervene as the interpreter, was carrying the household.

During her most recent case at court, she conferred with Police Sergeant Aldrich, who stopped by to witness a civil case of a friend of his. After the brief camaraderie of his greeting, Josie laid her predicament before him and implored him for any type of job Mike could avail himself.

"I'll let you know, Josie, I understand your predicament; I'll get to work on it right away."

"Anything at all, Bob, please!"

Mike had become a non-entity. He was no longer employed at the trade in which he excelled. He was penniless, and most demeaning of all, he could not provide for his daughter.

The appointment to apply for a position with the Philadelphia Police Force was looked upon as a miraculous blessing. Little did he imagine that it would be as a stablehand to groom horses and clear away their muck.

Josie waited to 'see what happens', until it was too late. Not even a disreputable doctor would perform an abortion on a pregnancy going into the second trimester. She would mother a child in her declining years during a depression.

Her mood swings were reverberating throughout the house. Irena stayed in her room. She rushed through her meals and ate very little. She was losing weight. Val continued to lend support, but he moved in with Eddie and Teresa. Mike was in a deep depression and was totally unaware of the situation surrounding him.

CHAPTER 48

LIFE GOES ON

The traditional daily prayer to the Blessed Mother, The Angelus, occurs three times a day at 6:00 a.m., noon, and at 6:00 p.m.

At Mass on Sundays, Josie began to identify her situation with that of the Virgin's… enduring an unexpected pregnancy. Her ironic sense of humor held small compensation under the pressure of her resentment.

Mike was too confused to contemplate suicide; he was barely aware of his own existence; something good had to happen.

Adrian received a long-distance phone call from a Stanley Slota, who needed to be in touch with Mike. The last communication reference Slota had was the Kaczynski market, where Mike was employed as a butcher. Adrian made a note of the name and contact number of the gentleman and gave the information to Val the next time he saw him.

Josie's hormones were dancing to their own tune. The infrequent calls to the magistrates' court and her current reticence to expose a neighboring alki-cooker left her with time on her hands in an empty house. Mike had taken to spending the nights in the police stable in Center City. He came home on his day off to wash his clothes and soak in a hot tub.

Irena isolated herself in her room. The only time Josie saw her was during breakfast and supper; there was little conversation - the two of them had nothing in common.

Josie's present condition and the futility of her economic status had her bordering on despair. She had to combat these issues. She became relentlessly tidy. Six to eight hours a day were spent scrubbing and dusting her way to exhaustion.

Val made it a point to deliver the phone message to Mike on his day off. Mike glanced at the slip of paper and put it in his pocket.

"Aren't you going to call?"

Mike waved his hand in a gesture that said, *Don't bother.*

"It might be important, Mike! He's your brother-in-law, isn't he?"

Mike shrugged his shoulders and walked away.

The weekly schedule listed Thursdays as 'launder bed linens' on Josie's itinerary. She had loaded her basket three times to carry the sheets and clothes to the basement. In the middle of wringing a sheet through the wringer, a sharp pain gripped her abdomen and held her in spasm. When it finally released its pressure, she left the sheet gripped between the wringers and went upstairs to phone the midwife.

At 10:45 a.m. on Thursday, October 13, 1932, an eight-pound baby girl was delivered to Mr. and Mrs. Szymborski. Neither parent had given much thought to a name; they didn't even consider the sex of the baby. They had been overwhelmed by the onus of an unwanted pregnancy and the effect that a newborn child would bring to their lives. They were middle-aged, trying to survive during an economic depression.

The midwife brought the baby to Josie, tidy and swaddled, "Here's your beautiful little girl. What's her name?"

The labor had been difficult for her, and she was still in pain. She tried to focus on the present moment, *Name, name, baby girl...* the radio on the bureau was playing an old-time favorite tune by Steven Foster, *"Jeanie with the Light Brown Hair."*

She reached for the baby, a warm feeling came over her, along with a warm smile, "Jeanie."

Val didn't bother to phone Mike - this was too important. He drove to Center City to pick him up.

Josie refused to let Mike near the baby until he bathed and changed clothes. Within fifteen minutes, he appeared in the door smelling of lye soap. He grabbed the baby and kissed every part of her little body, crying the whole time.

Her resentment cracked, and a feeling of sympathy and tenderness softened her approach.

"It's alright, Mike, we'll work something out."

Val was sitting in a chair next to Josie's bed; he eyed the scene skeptically.

"Mike, did you ever make that phone call?"

"Uh-uh, no."

"Put the baby back in the crib and come with me. There might be an opportunity for you. When was the last time you heard from him?"

"One, maybe two, yeah, two years ago."

Val dialed the operator to place a long-distance call to New York, then handed the phone to Mike.

"Stashek, it's me, Mike, you called?"

"Mike, I just about gave up on you. Listen, there's a possibility that you could get a job in the Astor Hotel, in the kitchen. They need an expert butcher like yourself."

Val overheard the conversation and grinned.

Monday, October 17th, Mike arrived at Times Square, New York for an interview with the kitchen manager of the Astor Hotel. Dressed in his dark blue serge business suit, starched white shirt, and dark blue tie sporting a Windsor knot, his dark gray Stetson completed the look of a successful businessman. He was Mike again.

CHAPTER 49

THE REAL McCOY

Philadelphia had become an 'open city.' Over 1,200 saloons operated openly. Over forty million dollars poured into the city every year. The city out-rivaled Chicago, New York, and Detroit in liquor sales. Corrupt politicians and the lax law enforcement contributed to the emergence of the bootlegging industry as the largest source of revenue in Philadelphia during the depression.

The end-of-the-year meeting of Charlie P's enterprise was held on board the Noah, the yacht that smuggled imported booze. Harvey Cuzak, owner of the Somers Point Restaurant, where the Noah made its berth, catered the affair; Canadian wine and Caribbean rum from the ship's hold embellished the tables.

Stabetski began the meeting with the blessing, an improvisation of a line he cribbed from the Yiddish text. "Oh, Heavenly Father, King of the Universe, who bestows the fruit of the vine, bless us here in our camaraderie and mutual endeavors." Making the sign of the cross, he continued, "In the name of the Father, the Son, and the Holy Ghost."

A jubilant "Amen" arose from the audience.

Charlie P rose from the center seat of the table to give the yearly accounting.

"First of all, I want to congratulate Trawinski. He was making a nice little side profit on the industrial liquor he was able to purchase under the guise of pharmaceutical requirements, which is untainted. This year, the deaths from tainted alcohol were well over two thousand. We're making enough profit from the sales of Canadian wine and the Real McCoy's rum. Our alki-cookers are standard ingredients sold only by Kaczynski and Dobrowski. God has blessed us. We provide a safe product that has caused no one any injury."

Bill McCoy ran a fleet of ships along Rum Row, a corridor that ran from Atlantic City to New York's Long Island, where his ships anchored just outside U.S. territorial waters. Boats belonging to enterprising bootleggers docked alongside to pick up pure, unadulterated rum shipped from the Caribbean. McCoy operated a risk-free business; no liquor left his boat without up-front payment. He never took bribes, and never involved himself in organized crime. The rum he purchase from the natives was undiluted and pure.

A rum toast went around the table, "This year our gross profit was over three-million dollars, coming in part from a hundred and sixty-five speakeasies."

CHAPTER 50

A NEW ERA

Franklin Delano Roosevelt's ancestral lineage and great wealth could have molded him into a privileged dandy, but his terrifying experience with poliomyelitis and his adventures with the poor people of Warm Springs, Georgia, prepared him to become one of the greatest presidents to hold office.

It was Josie's birthday, Saturday, March 4th, 1933. Valentine had presented her with a card containing five crisp one-hundred-dollar bills. A dozen red roses that Mike had sent her sat on the tea table in the living room within visual distance of her chair. The card read, "To my beautiful wife, *Sto lat."* Josie was alone. Irena had gone to New York to visit Mike, who was living with his brother-in-law in Brooklyn.

Josie was off alcohol while she nursed, a mug of coffee and a *pączki* sat on the end table. She was about to witness the inauguration of the new president; the proceedings were to be aired on the radio, nationwide, over all the networks.

Chief Justice Charles Evans Hughes administered the oath of office. The Roosevelt family Bible from 1686 lay open to 1 Corinthians 13.

Franklin Delano Roosevelt's first words;

"So, first of all, let me assert my firm belief that the only thing we have to fear…is fear itself. Our greatest primary task is to put people to work. There is no unsolvable problem if we face it wisely and courageously."

Mike made his usual appearance on Monday, his day off. Irena was not with him. Josie was in the kitchen and didn't hear him entering. When she came into the living room with a bottle of water for the baby, she found him standing beside the crib, sobbing with Regina in his arms. She didn't react. She didn't know what to make of it.

"Mike, what the hell's wrong with you?"

He wiped his nose with his hand, without looking up at her, "I'm here for Irena's and my things. She doesn't want to come back here."

Josie reacted, "What does this mean? Why are you taking your things?"

His eyes never left the baby's face, "My days are too busy to come here every week. I'll send you three dollars a week for the baby,"

He laid Jeanie in her crib, gave her a warm, paternal smile, then walked past Josie to go upstairs to pack.

Josie was reluctant to mention Mike's latest stunt to Val. He was helping Lucy and her. She couldn't swallow the guilt. Somehow, she would manage on the three dollars a week, bread was seven cents a loaf, and a quart of milk cost eleven cents. She and the baby would survive. The household bills could be covered by Val's birthday gift to her.

Val brought a canned ham and all the fixings for Easter dinner, along with a basket of colored eggs with a stuffed bunny for Jeanie. He also brought a bottle of rum to serve with the *bapka*. By the time they got to the *bapka*, Josie was feeling quite mellow.

"Have you heard anything from Mike?"

"No! That son-of-a-bitch has deserted us. He sends me three dollars a week to clear his conscience. If it wasn't for that five hundred dollars you gave me for my birthday, I'd be up shit's creek."

"Forget that bastard, Josie," he reached into his pocket and drew out his wallet, "Here's fifty dollars. Call a lawyer and get a divorce. I'll set you up with an alki-cooker and keep you supplied with the ingredients. You can live at home, like a lady, and earn your living."

Once the Thanksgiving parade was over, Philadelphia began to prepare for Christmas. Center City was wrapped in garlands and lights. Radio stations were playing *"Jingle Bells,"* and Bing Crosby was singing *"Silent Night."* The entire nation was putting their hopes in President Roosevelt's New Deal; things had to get better.

Another aspect of the new administration's agenda was to repeal the Volstead Act. The average working man would be able to step into a saloon and have a beer or two after ten to twelve hours of labor.

On December 5, 1933, Congress enacted the 21st Amendment to the Constitution, and the Volstead Act was repealed.

CHAPTER 51

SURVIVAL

The snow was deep, the temperature was low, but inside Charlie P's saloon, the Top Hat Trio was pumping out Christmas Carols in Polish and English. Every stool at the bar was taken, and young couples filled the tables. Mistletoe and Holly decorated the bar, the ceiling, and the walls. A wreath hung on the door, and Valentine Pancross was delighting the audience with his rich baritone voice.

Adjustments were in the making.

Ingredients for mash and alki-cookers were off the shelves. Income Tax was still the order of the day. Kaczynski's Grocery operated at a loss; Maya was dipping into her bootlegging cache. She was wearing down; she wanted out. But this was no time to sell. She would hang on until the economy was stable…if she lasted that long.

Dobrowski's Hardware was in the same predicament, but it was up to Kacper to keep the store going for his son Edward. He too would hang in for the long haul.

Trawinski had no options. Customers had become friends over the last twenty years. He carried their accounts on his books. Most of them could not afford their medication, some could not afford to eat. He would still carry them to the end.

Adam Stabetski, the man, and Adam Stabetski, the undertaker, were one and the same. There was no other way of life. People were still dying; people still needed to be buried in ceremony. The Polish people of Frankford and Bridesburg could not afford to pay for a decent meal, let alone a burial. Stabetski would remain the funeral director.

Valentine's cavalier style of living did not prepare him for the rainy day. What he didn't spend on himself, he spent on contributing to the household needs of his two sisters... and to treating his friends at the bar.

Matczek competently ran Charlie's saloon, so there was no reason to add Val to the payroll. Val did, however, maintain weekend gigs to entertain the customers along with Steve Leonik. Val was unemployed.

Stabetski always appreciated Val's looks, his carriage, and most of all, his baritone voice. Val was an expert driver. He had driven in and out of situations that other men could scarcely imagine. Val had charisma... and he had a voice that was soothing and pleasant to hear. Also, he cut a handsome figure in the chauffeur's uniform.

His Friday and Saturday night gigs at Charlie P's added to his weekly income; he could make it comfortably.

Loss of the alki-cooker placed Josie right back where she started. Three dollars a week support money from Mike ensured food on the table, but it did not allow for household bills. Commission calls at court from the Pilsudski Union were non-existent. Val could no longer be a provider. She existed.

By March, her utility bills were in arrears, and her house was up for Sheriff Sale. Val ached to help her. He even tried to borrow money from the network, but everyone was looking out for themselves.

Breakfast at the Stabetski table was a routine occurrence. Upcoming funeral details were discussed over omelets and coffee.

Val's usual bright and witty remarks were replaced with a sullen, bleak demeanor. His unusual attitude went overlooked by Stabetski, but Wanda instinctively knew Val was confronting an unpleasant issue that he could not resolve.

"Valenti, what's bothering you? You are not your usual self?"

Val shrugged it off, "Nothing."

"Oh, it must be something! I'll not move from this table until you tell me what this dark problem is. It often helps to talk about problems confronting us. So, tell me. What could make you this sad?"

Stabetski got up from his chair, "I'll see you in the office when Wanda is finished with you."

"Val?"

"It's Josie, Wanda. She's losing her home and there's no way I can help her. She wants to get out of there before they paste the notice on the door, and she has nowhere to go with the baby."

Wanda looked down at her plate. There was another time when Josie was facing domestic issues. Wanda had provided her with a job and a babysitter; she did well in her role as provider. Josie was once again in crisis, this time with a baby to care for.

"Valenti, one thing we have in this house are spare rooms. Bring Josie and the baby here, and they will be safe."

Fortunately, with the three dollars a week from Mike, Josie was able to pay for her food and small necessities.

Violet was upset over the loss of the home that she was raised in. Josie's relationship with Mike had caused a rift between them, but the knowledge that her mother was homeless and with a new baby to care for tied her in knots. That she could in no way alleviate her mother's distress had a daunting effect on her, one that she could not shake.

George did what he could to assuage her moodiness without success. He was uncomfortable with the situation and tried to explain to his parents that Violet needed their support and understanding. Josie's situation was a dark cloud that could not be ignored.

The monthly meeting of the Horn & Hardart managers was held in the Horn Building on 16th and Chestnut Streets. During the coffee break, Dimitri Kryszostoff overheard a conversation between the manager of the building and the chief of Human Resources. Another elevator operator was needed for the building.

Dimitri edged his way over to the pair and, as politely as he could, asked, "Does the person have to be a licensed operator?"

The building manager was taken aback. He tilted his head and looked directly in Dimitri's eye, "There's a two-week orientation program for either an experienced operator or a novice.

After all, there's not much effort required in turning the wheel. It's a matter of personal demeanor, offering service with a smile."

Dimitri reached for his hand, gave it a firm shake and offered a genuine smile, "I have just the person you need." He looked at the chief of Human Resources, "She is a mature woman with a good work background. Her name is Josephine Szymborska. I'll write it down for you."

Josie was very discerning in choosing her wardrobe. She selected her best gray business suit that she wore in her role as interpreter, her black and white Spectator pumps, a little black hat hugged her head, her black leather purse, and her best white gloves completed the ensemble. A look in the full-length mirror gave her the confidence to make the trip to 16th and Chestnut Street.

She was waiting at the door of Human Resources in the Horn Building when the door was opened.

Her new job paid nine dollars a week. She offered to pay Wanda three dollars a week for the room until she could find an apartment, but Wanda refused.

"I know how responsible you are, Josephine, but I don't need the money, and you could use it for your application for an apartment. Good luck in your search."

Val's newfound work ethic began to drag on him. The full-time position at Stabetski's and his weekend gig at Charlie's weighed him down.

The Blue Law of Pennsylvania kept bars and saloons from conducting business as usual on Sundays. However, private clubs were exempt. Val soon became a card-carrying member of the Slovak Social Club on Fairmount Avenue, a former Speakeasy on his illicit alcohol route.

This is where he heard about a large, comfortable apartment over the Weinstein Pharmacy on Fifth and Fairmount Streets. The kitchen had modern appliances, and a deck overlooked a large Buttonwood tree. It was perfect for Josie, and much closer to her new job.

Charlie P was pleased to hear of Josie's good fortune and picked up the tab for the move, plus three months' rent in advance.

The tide had turned for Josie. Everything was going her way, with the only kink in the upcoming arrangements being the acute need of a babysitter. It was an inconvenience for Ludja to travel the distance, and her arthritis limited her mobility. This issue had to be resolved immediately.

Val brought the issue at hand to the bar of the Slovak Social Club,

"My sister is moving into the apartment over the drug store. She needs a babysitter for her year-old daughter. Anybody know someone?"

Frank Nekoranick spoke up, "I have an eighteen-year-old daughter who can't find a job. What's the pay?"

Val took it on himself, "Three dollars!" Josie could afford two dollars, and he'd chip in the other dollar.

On Easter Sunday, Josie tied the ribbons of a brand new bonnet under Jeanie's chin. She was grateful to God and wanted to pay him a personal visit. The Slovak Church was just three blocks away, an easy stroll.

An usher was standing in front of the one-story church building, holding the large oak door open for the incoming parishioners. He greeted everyone with the universal, "Hallelujah!"

Josie immediately felt the warmth of the small sanctuary with three altars and all the right statues sitting on pedestals. She remembered her place as an excommunicated Catholic and chose an end seat on the last row. She was spiritually involved with the service until Communion was served; the looks of annoyance on the faces of the people trying to slide by her knees on the way to the altar initiated a firm resolve in her never to return to church again.

CHAPTER 52
FORTUITY

Val no longer filled his flask with vodka to pull him through a funeral; the extreme heat and humidity of July required constant hydration, so he instead filled his flask with water.

Stabetski's entire quarters were fitted with air-conditioning. Val looked forward to the routine information breakfast. Coffee was served, and the cook prepared omelets and toast. Val glanced at the statistics on the 3 by 5 index card, "Walter Goniek,"

Val stifled a cough; he had a bar-friend at the Slovak Social Club named Walter Goniek, a handsome young man, maybe twenty-five. He was shocked. He checked the date of birth, 11 February 1877. Val sighed and a smile played on his lips, it must be the father.

Val was seated in a chair next to the small organ in the reception room. He and the organist had just finished reviewing the hymns that would be sung that evening for the wake of Walter Goniek, Sr.

His friend, the young Walter Goniek, arrived holding his mother's arm as she slowly made her way to the chair where she would sit to greet the viewers. She was a short, plump woman with a round face and a permed head of brown hair; she looked to be in her late forties.

Walter noticed Val and gave a brief nod.

At the reception, after the funeral, Val sat with the Goniek family: Walter, his wife, Marian, and his mother, Stefcha. He ingratiated himself, paying particular attention to the widow, who, he learned, was left with a sizable insurance grant at her husband's demise.

The following Sunday night at the Slovak Social Club, Val made every effort to engage Walter Goniek in song and drink, to comfort him due to his recent loss. Val invested his entire paycheck on Walter's favorite drink, Grand Marnier.

By two o'clock, closing time, it was obvious, Walter did not have the mobility or the coherence to get him across Fairmount Avenue. Val assured the president of the club, Frank Yankovich, that he would safely tuck Walter into his bed.

"You know you can count on me, Frank." There was a sobering assurance in his tone. Frank nodded his head and helped him down the stairs.

Val spent the night on the Goniek's sofa and was there for a *kielbasa* breakfast. Stefcha doted on him. He had gone out of his way to bring her son safely home.

"Could you come back, Valenti, for dinner today? I have a beautiful eye-roast of beef with *pierogi*."

Walter tittered, "And a bottle of Grand Marnier!"

From then on, Val made it his business to drop in on the Goniek's on his weekly visits to the Slovak Social Hall, just across the street. He soon became one of the family. He entertained them with songs and funny stories. He paid particular interest in the grieving widow and soon captured her heart. He became a household member, and in time, resigned his position at Stabetski's because Stefcha found the position demeaning to her talented and handsome consort.

CHAPTER 53
RESOLUTION

Peace and Brotherhood?

1945 was a year of monumental change. A cerebral hemorrhage took the life of President Franklin Delano Roosevelt on 12 April 1945. Vice President Harry S. Truman became the thirty-third President of the United States.

After six years of conflict, four of which involved the United States, the European conflict of World War II ended with the surrender of Germany on May 8, 1945.

Now that the European Stage of the conflict was resolved, there was a sense of wrapping things up—getting the war in the Pacific to end and peace would reign once more over the globe.

Harry S. Truman made the ultimate decision, and the Los Alamos scientific experiment with nuclear fission was completed. The end products, two atomic bombs, were transported by ship aboard the USS Indianapolis, which was sunk by a Japanese submarine just after delivering to Tinian Naval Base its ultra-secret payloads - dubbed the "Fat Man" and the "Little Boy."

"Little Boy" was craftily fitted onto the *"Enola Gay,"* a Boeing B-29 Bomber, which dropped its payload over Hiroshima on the sixth of August. When Japan refused to surrender, it was followed by another operationally successful but horrific bombing by the B-29, *"Bock's Car,"* delivering the "Fat Man" over Nagasaki on August 9, 1945.

An estimated 140,000 people were obliterated in Hiroshima, with a further 74,000 people decimated in Nagasaki.

Emperor Hirohito of Japan finally capitulated and signed the Imperial Surrender pact on 2 September 1945.

Now that millions of lives had been lost, and cities and towns in the Atlantic and Pacific zones were destroyed, the global leaders of the world decided to get together and ensure that such devastation should never recur.

The United Nations was established on October 24, 1945.

The rows and rows of brick homes in Philadelphia were occasionally softened by a tall tree offering shade in the summer. In 1945, fall made an early visit, and the Poplar trees changed the color of their leaves in mid-September. The Oaks followed suit in October, but the Buttonwood tree that stood outside the apartment on Fifth and Fairmount would hold onto its green leaves and brown buttons throughout the winter.

It was Jeanie's thirteenth birthday, and puberty was having its way with her. Josephine made sure that her school uniform was clean and pressed, but there were days when her daughter left for school with barely running a brush through her hair; she was much in need of refinement.

Elsa Bauer had an eye for fashion. Elsa was at Wanamaker's shopping for an appealing dress for her adopted niece, Jeanie. Josie and she had made plans for a surprise party that would be held at Richman's Ice Cream Parlor, where Mrs. Richman was prepared to participate in the event.

Jeanie rushed through her Saturday morning chores. The Philadelphia Eagles were playing the Cleveland Rams, the leading team. Steve Van Buren, 'Supersonic Steve', the powerful Eagle's fullback, was her idol. Since he was drafted by the NFL in 1944, she hadn't missed a game. She had the radio and the living room to herself, as Josie was in the basement, busy with the weekly laundry. The doorbell rang, a commercial was on, so Jeanie jumped out of her seat to run downstairs; they rarely had visitors.

A uniformed messenger stood waiting at the door, clipboard in hand, his bicycle propped against his body, "Telegram for Josephine Pancross."

"She's not here," Jeanie lied, "I'm her daughter, can I sign for it?"

He shrugged his shoulders and handed her the clipboard.

She scrawled her name and snatched the telegram. She shut the door and ran downstairs to the basement.

"You got a telegram!"

Josie let go of the wringer lever, a scowl on her face, "Who the hell would be sending me a telegram?"

The message read, "Mike passed away, 5 September 1945." It was signed Stanley Slota.

"Your father is dead!"

Jeanie raised her head to acknowledge the information, then turned to run back upstairs. *Had the Eagles scored?*

"Where do you think you're going?"

She threw an incredulous look her way, "Upstairs to listen to the Eagles," and in a self-righteous manner added, "It's my birthday, I get to do what I want!"

"Not until you take this basket of dried clothes up with you."

"Alright!" she snapped.

"Fold them and put them away."

"Shit!" she murmured.

The laundry was finished, the bathroom and bedrooms were cleaned, fresh linens were on the bed, and Josie was in the shower when Aunt Elsa arrived carrying packages.

"Happy birthday, Jeanie!" She gave her a hug and kissed the top of her head. Jeanie gave her a squeeze and an expectant smile.

"Here, open this one first."

The bow was pulled off, the paper ripped away, the lid of the box thrown on the side, tissue spread open, and a pale lavender dress of a simple but mature design was pulled from the box.

"Oh, thank you, Aunt Elsa, I love it. Do you mind if I try it on?"

"I can't wait to see it on you."

Josie heard the exchange and entered the living room to see what the excitement was about. Her face softened, and her voice was tender, "You look beautiful. Wait, I have something to go with that."

She returned holding a small package topped with a blue ribbon, the contents of which could only be a ring. She handed it to Jeanie to unwrap.

A 14 karat gold ring was embedded in the tiny slot, the initials JAS were etched on a signet-style ring. Josie had taken her wedding ring to the jewelers and had it resized to fit Jeanie's right ring finger.

The tables at Richman's at 2:00 p.m. were empty. Cheeseburgers were ordered and served. Josie let loose some emotional stuff.

"This is a strange day. Jeanie's birthday and the news of Mike's death," she laid her burger down, her thoughts took center stage. "I will go to confession next Saturday and make myself right with the Lord. *Dzięki Bogum,* I will receive communion on Sunday for the first time in fifteen years. My life is just beginning."

Mrs. Richman pushed through the folding doors of the kitchen, carrying a candle-lit birthday cake. The few customers in the shoppe joined in on the birthday song as Jeanie blew out the candles.

The world was at peace. Elsa was about to become a grandmother by her eldest son. Josie was a free woman, and Jeanie would soon be a freshman in Little Flower High School.

It was, indeed, the beginning of a new era.

About the Author...

Regina A. McIntyre is a Polish-American author of five historical fiction novels. She was born in Brooklyn, NYC and raised in Philadelphia, Pennsylvania, Her novels are all historically based, exhaustively researched and well known for holding sacrosanct the history and factual elements of the eras her stories are set in.

Her four previous novels are as follows:

Altar of Sod (2010)- As the nineteenth century comes to a close in Partioned Poland, the village of Miscka sits almost unchanged on the banks of the Vistula River. This is the story of three families unforgettably joined by love, pain, struggles, and hope. The story unfolds against a rich tapestry of Polish ceremony and tradition and builds to a far reaching climax.

Yesterday's Pupils (2010) - At the turn of the Twentieth Century, three families emigrate from the same village in Poland to Philadelphia. This book describes how their lives and attitudes change as they adjust to the dynamic industrial and cultural influence of this historic era.

Resistance (2022) - On the night of 31 August 1939, the word 'blitzkrieg' was added to the dictionary. The German Luftwaffe was discharging incendiary bombs from the sky, while the Wehrmacht stormed the ground with heavy artillery. The Polish Army made a valiant effort, but they were outweighed in machinery, munitions, and manpower. By 14 September, the invading forces had them surrounded. There was no way out. The final defeat of Poland took place in a marshy area of the Bug River. The document of surrender was signed 6 October 1939. The Poles never accepted the term *"Unconditional."*

Rising (2024) - **The sequel to *Resistance*.** This compelling and spellbinding novel is set against the ill-fated Warsaw Uprising. Historically accurate to the drama's most definable details, it encompasses a gut-wrenching tale of the many heroic lives impacted by this rising of war-weary Poles against their oppressive overlords, the Nazi forces of Adolf Hitler's Germany. Once initiated, they find their dire situation is rapidly and catastrophically manipulated by Stalin's Soviet Forces, who stand pat only to observe from the far banks of the Vistula River.

Published Proudly by
DAMTE Associates Publishing LLC
Cartersville, Georgia 30120